THE LAST CROSSING

Badriya Al-Badri

The Last Crossing (Novel)

Originally published as *'Aloboor Alakir'*

Translated by: Katherine Van de Vate

© 2024 Dar Arab For Publishing and Translation LTD.

United Kingdom
60 Blakes Quay
Gas Works Road
RG1 3EN
Reading
United Kingdom
info@dararab.co.uk
www.dararab.co.uk

First Edition 2024
ISBN 978-1-78871-099-2
Copyrights © dararab 2024

Text Edited: Marcia Lynx Qualey
Text Design: Nasser Al Badri
Cover Design: Hassan Almohtasib

BADRIYA AL-BADRI

The Last Crossing

A NOVEL

TRANSLATED BY BY KATHERINE VAN DE VATE

Dramatis Personae

In Mukhtar's village

Houria: Mukhtar's cousin and the love of his life

Am Abd al-Razzaq and Khaleh Karimah

Amjad

Shaykh Yassin

At the construction site

Ahmad, Ajay, Babu, Ihsan Akbar, and Rampir: Mukhtar's co-workers

Kumar Kapoor: Manager

Sanjay: Foreman

At the date farm

Am Sulayman: Owner of the date farm

Taj al-Islam: Mukhtar's supervisor

At the café

Abdullah: Mukhtar's roommate while he is working in the cafe

Hajj Salih: Proprietor of the cafe

At the furniture workshop

Marwan, Mujahid, and Tawfiq: Mukhtar's co-workers

Shaykh Mansur: Proprietor of the furniture workshop

Chapter One

The Accident

Five years after Mukhtar arrives in Oman

Your first step in life is your first step on the road to death.

Lights are running toward me. It is the first time I've seen lights with legs. It is not a cartoon; these are real lights, running so fast they are panting, their tongues lolling out, drooling as if they are about to leap on someone and shred him with their sharp fangs. I try to run away, but I can't find my legs. Oh God, did I forget them when I went out? Didn't I put them on before my shoes? Could I have left them on deposit with one of the market peddlers who crowd the street, hawking contraband goods? Did a peddler steal them—maybe the one selling cheap leather shoes? Yes, it must have been him. His shoes were so shabby he was forced to steal my feet, their cracks showing through my open-toed shoes, though I had worn long rough woollen socks to hide my chapped feet. But what will he do with my feet? Maybe it was my new shoes he wanted. Why didn't he just ask for them? I would have been glad to hand them over for nothing; I might even have bought a new pair from him. That way, he could have killed two birds with one stone, instead of taking both my shoes and my feet.

Could it have been the sardine-seller? I always saw him sloshing barefoot through red pools of ice-melt from the frozen fish, a clear sign that he was used to blood. Damn him! He doesn't know I pass out at the touch of blood, let alone a stroll through it. When I was a child, I would faint if I saw blood trickling from a cut in my finger or a gash in my forehead, like the one I got when I fell out of a tree. Its branch gave way beneath me when I climbed up to play with a bird's nest and broke its brown-speckled eggs; the spots were all different, except for their colour, and the eggs were about to hatch.

I was forever getting into scrapes like these when I skipped Shaykh Yassin's lessons in hopes of avoiding his cane, which invariably found its way to my back because I hadn't memorized Surat al-Shams, Surat al-A'la, or even Surat al-Bayyinah. Though the Shaykh swore a mere infant could master al-Bayyinah, I couldn't seem to lodge its verses in the deepest corner of my soul, a place I have never reached, that I am not even sure exists. The only Surah I memorized, almost before Shaykh Yassin had finished reciting it, was al-Ikhlas. My hand shot up as I shouted jubilantly:

"Me, Shaykh Yassin, me, me!"

Once again, he aimed his cane at me as he intoned Surat al-A'raf:

"'So when the Qur'an is recited, listen and be quiet, that you may be granted mercy.' How many times do I have to repeat it before you understand?"

But I still insisted on reciting, and my delight in that moment, as my classmates watched me surreptitiously, gave rise to a happiness that has lasted my entire life. I was so thrilled I even forgot the sting of the Shaykh's cane, though it left its mark just below my left shoulder where he directed it before stowing it beside him. Shaykh Yassin did not forget to tell my father about my achievement so my father would reward him for his efforts with me, but my father gave me an even bigger sum to express his pride in his clever son, advising me not to tell Shaykh Yassin lest he take offence. And, like a little man sworn to guard his father's secret, I have told no one until this day.

I used to play truant and fritter away the day until it was time to go home, so my mother would not discover I had not gone to memorize the Qur'an. I would climb trees to pick the dangling fruit their owner had intended to give to his own children or abandon myself to the irrigation ditch, where mud settled on my body until my mother's loofah attacked it like an enemy to be repelled.

The lights are running, running, but I stand rooted like a tree, staring into death's face. All I can do is freeze where I am and take refuge in my pounding heart, its beats deafening me to what is happening around me. The lights draw closer, blinding me, not giving me a chance even to peek at them. I close my eyes tightly and press my lids, concentrating all my strength in them. I turn my entire body away from the lights and try to hide, clamping my knees together, wrapping my arms around them, and doubling up as if performing an extra prostration to strengthen my prayers.

At last I find my feet. So I didn't forget them at home, and no peddler stole them, not even the vendor of used clothes, which are carefully ironed after being washed all together in an old tub on an abandoned farm. The stains clinging to the clothes reveal they were laundered clumsily, hastily, without regard to the rules for health and safety. Anyway, why should these vendors trouble to protect us from disease and death? We are but passers-by, looking over their goods before moving on, rarely buying anything that might motivate them to take care of us. If one of us does buy something, his skin and blood had better be used to infection, so he won't lie awake all night worrying about it. We don't fear the appearance of spots on our bodies that the blazing sun has blackened, so what do a few pustules matter? We no longer distinguish between the itch of a skin infection, sunburn, or even the bites of the mosquitos that feed on our blood, immune to its poison. How often we heard the taunt, "Don't be soft like a woman!" when we tried to scratch what those clothes left on our "effeminate bodies", as the vendors mocked when one of us had an allergic reaction. That is why their businesses will always turn a profit.

I try to lift my feet, but they are still stuck to the sidewalk. Will an apple fall and save me from this fearsome gravity before it kills me? Why won't my body move? Won't the force of the light that is headed for me move it? Well then, Mr. Newton, since you have failed in your theory that for every action, there is an equal and opposite reaction, let Mr. Einstein come and rescue me from this assault of spacetime, since the velocity of objects can't exceed the speed of light. Maybe the light speeding toward me will transfer its tremendous force to my body so I can start running before the lights gobble me up, before I become a tender morsel for them, or nothing at all. I don't know what will happen if I can't lift my feet right away.

Not even the math and physics that I loved, at which I excelled, can save me now. Everything is slipping away: my pride in my mastery of both theoretical and applied physics, the hand that was holding mine but has let it go. Now I am alone, facing lights that hate me for some unknown reason. My left hand clutches my ticket home, while my right holds that of a friend, who drops it the moment he sees the lights that are hell-bent on getting me. And if a friend's hand fails during life's first test, how could it have been the hand that woke you before dawn to earn a living? How could it have joined you for Friday prayers in the city where you had finally settled after years of wandering in torment from one village to another, from the injustice of one city to the pandemonium of another, before you were tossed like a tasty morsel into the jaws of a third that will never tire of chewing up your spirit?

My eyes can barely see; in fact, I can't see a thing. My eyes are filled with the white all around me. I have to make a decision before the lights reach me and take what they want. I have to flee, throw my spirit to the winds, run as fast as I can, maybe even faster. I'm so light I can't control my body, moving so fast that my body is rising from the ground, as if reacting at last to the speeding lights. Rest in peace now, Einstein; your theory was correct. The physics I loved has not let me down, and I did not memorize its laws for nothing. If my mother could see me now, she would forget how she used to reproach me for spending more time studying physics than memorizing the Qur'an or learning the prayers and devotions that could protect me when something evil comes upon me, like a light that hates me for reasons I don't understand.

I close my eyes. My mother's image comes to me. She raises her clasped hands toward the sky and entreats God, her voice breathless and quavering, to bring me back so she may rest her eyes on me and my children. How often she had dreamt their shouting would fill her house as she chased after them with her broad cane, brandishing it as they recoiled, before everyone broke out laughing, secure in the knowledge that the kind-hearted grandmother was only picking a quarrel so as to draw them into her warm lap and the stories she never tired of repeating.

By the age of seven, we had memorized all her tales—of Clever Hasan, Antar and his beloved Abla, and the prince transformed into a frog by an evil witch, his only salvation the love of a girl willing to marry a frog. What a silly story, as ridiculous as the one about the good witch who turned a poor orphan into a princess and helped her marry the prince she met at the ball, which he had organized to find a wife of whom his eyes would never tire, from whom he could not bear to be parted. No sooner had he seen her than he fell in love and chose her to share his throne, not caring that she was an impoverished orphan.

My poor mother! What a good soul she is. She doesn't realize the poor were not created for love and there is no such thing as a good witch. In her latest message, she sent me her voice, filled with exhaustion from having no one to confide in. She told me she feared death would take her before my return, and she was frightened by the dream that had kept her awake two nights before—a vision of me riding on the wing of a giant bird, like the roc in the stories of Sindbad, but even bigger. Then she urged me to take care of Houria, our neighbours' daughter. I had hoped Houria would share my life, but she refused to be anything but a wound I could not heal.

If Houria only knew how I long to embrace her now, to shout at the top of my voice:

I love you. Forgive me for running away after you brushed me from your heart as if you were dusting off your chic blue dress, which you wore like a queen unrivalled on her throne. Dust loves to spread itself on dark colours, but it isn't happy on your clothing, where your two small hands with their short slender fingers attack it at the least approach. My God! How grateful I would have been to those hands, so thin their bones protruded, if they had taken mine at that moment and held fast, if you had not let go of that man weak in everything but loving you. If only you had not looked away from me as I knelt before you in abject humility.

Give me your hands now; let us fly away together. The sky is vast, and I cannot bear it alone; I am frightened of its enormity. You know I can't stand the heights that you adore. More than once my heart nearly stopped when you insisted on taking the dangerous high rides at the fairground. I had to go with you; I had to join in your recklessness and protect you from any harm that might befall you up there, far from me. This happened often when we were children, when I was your safe harbour, and you were my whole universe. I wonder if my chest would be crushed by fear now if you were here with me, laughing as you used to on those "death rides," as I called them, since only a whisker seemed to separate us from death. They would lift us into the seventh heaven before plummeting at insane speeds into the bowels of the earth, which was ready to embrace our scattered remains, shattered beyond all repair, if even one tiny screw were to come loose.

That's enough talk of rides. Linking them to my current state is just a vain attempt to hang on to life. Did I say life? What life do I mean? Was it the one I wanted with you? Our children who won't go to sleep until we've told them three bedtime stories at least, so I take them to my mother's house, since her voice is a river of stories? You smile when I return alone after leaving them with her so I can savour a tasty meal fit for a lover. The rutted road to our house—how can I complain of its roughness when it leads me to you? The laughter we will share, occasionally pausing to face each other like fighters taking a break from combat, only to laugh even harder? Can you remember why we're laughing? You can't? Me neither. Never mind; let's laugh and forget those idle proverbs that claim it's rude to laugh for no reason. If we don't laugh at life, it will laugh at us.

If only I'd had the life I wanted with you. Instead, I am trapped in the life to which you banished me, imprisoned in it, and you could not have borne to live it with me. Where has your voice gone? Why doesn't it come to me, hoarse and cold as ice, like it was when you said: "I'm sorry. You have to think of the future before thinking of marriage; you have to build yourself up and show me you can give me a decent life before I consider binding myself to you. I don't want the life I have now. Why don't you go to work in one of the Gulf countries so you can return with your dreams in your hands? Then

I'll seriously think of marrying you. I'm making no promises. I don't deny I love you, but who knows? Maybe it's not love; maybe I'm just used to having you around. Love isn't enough to build a house or make dreams a reality. You understand what I mean, of course."

Houria, you turned your back on love and left. That day was the first time I had stood in front of you without seeing you, as if my eyes were clouded by fragments of sleep. I counted the grains of sand frozen on the pavement and the leaves that the trees had discarded beneath my feet as if they were laughing at me—me, the one you had discarded from your blood, whom no one could put back together. I remember how I swallowed my tears for fear that passersby would cluster around me like flies around uncovered food or a rotting corpse. Which was I, the uncovered food or a rotting corpse? Never mind; it's not important. Flies will gather whether I ask them for a reason or try to swat them away.

What if I hadn't let you leave me, reject me, with no say in the matter? What if I had run after you and pleaded by everything you held dear to show me mercy? "Bring me back to life, don't leave without at least turning around to see the effect of your crime. Don't criminals always return to the scene to make sure they've left no trace? Why don't you come back and see the trace your departure won't erase? I want to cry out to you; I open my mouth to shout: "Stop, Houria, for heaven's sake, stop! I will die if you don't come back, I will...".

My father's face appears before me. Since his recent death, my life has been hard. He stands there as he did when I was small, when he would upbraid me for crying after Amjad, our neighbours' son, hit me and took my new ball, refusing to let me play with it. Though he was only two years my senior, Amjad seemed ten years older because he was so big and I so small. Though he was rich and owned more than anyone else in our neighbourhood, Amjad always coveted what others had. Standing in front of me, my father says:

"You are a man, and men don't cry. Lower your voice and smile; have faith that she'll come back to you. One day she'll come to you, and you will reject her. Don't cry—crying doesn't suit love."

Who told you, father, that crying doesn't suit love? For once, I will ignore your advice. Forgive me, father, I scream, but I can't hear my voice. I try to cling to something, anything, but there is only air and nothingness. My hands grope in great expanses of emptiness; darkness swirls around me like a relentless tornado. I raise my voice again but hear only the echo of silence. I turn toward my father, who is smiling and pointing at something in his hand: "I've told you before," he says. "Men don't cry."

Chapter Two

The Construction Site

Mukhtar's first year in Oman

The mirror doesn't lie. When you stand before it, it tells you just what you have gained and what you have lost.

Houria

These days I don't dream of much. I dream only of waking to your kiss on my forehead for dawn prayers, or racing to the kitchen before you to make a quick breakfast to carry our bodies through a long day, or tucking a poem I wrote earlier into your shirt pocket for you to read when you are overcome by longing for me, as you review plans for the building your company is constructing. I dream of leaving you a note on yellow paper, in the shape of an untouched apple, that I attach to the fridge door with a smiley-faced magnet winking its left eye. The magnet is yellow, too, since it's my favourite colour, as you know.

I love you

Remember to bring home mulberries

Your son craves them

And also, don't forget:

I love you.

I imprint a kiss on the paper with my orange lipstick, the colour of a ripe peach, a colour you used to love. I put the note on the fridge and let my footsteps take me far from your promised paradise. I dream of getting home from work before you to fix a delicious lunch to vanquish your fatigue and hunger, as well as the Om Ali you always brought to our house, pretending it was from your mother.

Do you remember? I want to weep whenever your sister Sawsun brings us a bowlful of your mother's Om Ali. All your mother knows is that I have always loved her Om Ali; she doesn't realize I no longer eat it. When I look at it, all I can see is your smile on its surface, and I am overcome by sobs. Then I take the bowl that my brothers have licked clean back to my aunt Umm Mukhtar, thanking her and asking her to fix it always, since no one makes it like she does. She embraces me tearfully: "With all my heart, light of my eyes! May God bring Mukhtar back so I can rejoice in your children before I die. Be patient, my daughter, Mukhtar will come back soon."

Your mother still hopes I will marry her emigré son. She doesn't realize he's banished me from his heart and sentenced me to oblivion; he's replaced his love for me with a hatred my heart finds hard to bear. Nor does she realize I am not waiting for your return but for a message from you, even a blank one, to reassure me that, one day, there may again be a place for me in your heart. That day will be brightened by the butterflies that fluttered from my hands as they waved at the wounds that took you far away from me.

Thank God, I know you are safe when I see you have received my texts. Every message from me means another bruise from you and a distance between us that keeps growing until I can no longer measure it. It is as if we live on separate planets or we were created in an earlier era, and our exhausted souls have had the misfortune to meet again, only to suffer the same exhaustion. Don't some people believe in reincarnation, when the souls of those who died in one era migrate to the bodies of those living in another? The proof of this is that we are often not surprised by new experiences; it seems as though we've lived through them before. Or when we hear a story for the first time, we secretly believe that it is not new, that we have already heard it. Nothing is new except for this ever-growing pain that we reject, that is as raw as when we first encountered it. Never mind. I can put up with all of this. It is the price of my vanity; all it did was take me away from you before I came crawling back, as you slammed the door in my face and shouted that I no longer deserve your heart.

This hand reflected in the mirror was the one that dried my tears last night. Exhausted by my longing for you, I felt my heart dissolve into my veins. When my father saw my swollen eyes, I told him I'd had an asthma attack. I couldn't bring myself to confess I am strangling on a love that grows faster than I can contain, a love equalled only by the distance between us.

Since you left, I have taken to standing in front of the mirror every day, when it tells me what I have gained and what I have lost. Today was no different. For the thousandth time, I said the same thing and heard the same response. Nothing has changed. You are you, and I am me. Neither of us can overcome our fear or pass through the needle's eye of love. I consider rebelling; I glance at your eyes in the mirror; I waver and meekly submit, but the lump remains stuck in my throat, as it has a thousand and one times before.

I scrutinize my face as if poring through the pages of a book I'll never finish reading. There is a dark spot on my right cheek. It appeared the day you left, and I have been unable to cover it up ever since. It reminds me of all the pain you thrust so thoughtlessly between my ribs. The spots dotting my chin as if I were a teenage girl who has just realized she is maturing merely show my constant fear that you won't return; they are further marks of the anxiety that has carved its dark circles beneath my eyes.

I no longer care about the mascara I finally learned to wear. In any case, I only wore for you; I didn't care about it before. My recent trip to the beauty salon and the little wounds from plucking my eyebrows are not important. Nobody will notice them, and nobody cares. The red lipstick emphasizing the curve of my lower lip; the hair I have finally cut off because long hair doesn't suit an unhappy woman. My smile? What can I say? It's a stranger to me these days.

I decide to stop reading and start writing instead. Picking up a tube of dark red lipstick, I write "Mukhtar" at the top of my mirror, leaving your name suspended there, like our fate, and go away. But I return to sit in front of the mirror, my chin resting on my palms, trying to immerse myself in those two eyes, to read them. I imagine I see you in their depths, I speak to you, embrace your eyes, but as usual, you remain silent, until you finally pull me to you and say:

"I love you, Houria. Why do you love me so much now that I'm gone?"

I close my eyes and reply: "Why do I love you so much, Mukhtar, now that you're gone?"

We've traded places. Now, I understand completely how you felt all those times I looked at you so nonchalantly, throwing my insouciance in your face. I was determined to goad you, to keep you as a lover on call whom I never summoned. I admit that whenever I saw love blazing in your eyes, my joy increased, and when I felt your weakness, I grew stronger inside. The greater your love, the more I pushed it away. A hateful woman nested inside me like a devil, delighting as she watched you burn in hell.

You die a thousand times without dying. Each time God replaces your heart with one that beats only for the love of me. You are like a sinner overtaken by death, with no chance to repent. You were guilty only of a love that wore its purity like rags, a love for which no one interceded in the face of my monstrous conceit. Don't you think it is fair I'm now suffering as you did, burning in the same hell to which I sent you, torturing myself to please you, while you turn away from me as from a mangy dog not good enough to give a drink of water, even as you watch him pant with thirst?

Never mind, Mukhtar. One day we will meet again, and you will see that the broken woman now writing to you is the one who once spurned you.

Mukhtar

The sound of your message was faint, unlike your face, which greeted me as I stumbled in my effort to string together my words, to whisper that I love you. Was it wintertime, my bones and fingers trembling as I rubbed them to get warm, or was summer lashing my face, damp with sweat and tears, as you mocked my heart that had flung itself at your feet, only for you to kick it?

You know what I suffered, you say? No, my dearest, there's a world of difference between the one who leaves and the one who is left, between she who decides and he who submits. We are alike only in that when we chose, we both chose you. When we wept, we both wept for you. Apart from that, there is no comparison. It was you who rose into the sky and looked down on me from your ivory tower. The higher you rose, the smaller I appeared in your eyes, though it was I who once competed with dreams to make you happy, drawing lanterns of starlight for your eyes, their light bouncing back at me like a meteor, I who forged necklaces of joy for your breast, and collars that you clamped around my neck.

When I said "I love you", the letters didn't race to my lips, but flew from my veins to yours, without my trying to stop or even slow them. I know now that I made the wrong decision; that my heart, unfit for love after you left, was like a truculent child, throwing stone after stone at the face of fear to reach you. The problem, my love, is that our hearts write in ink, not pencil, and any attempt to erase what they've written only smudges it, may God help us.

"Mukhtar! Get over here now so the sun doesn't fry us before we finish moving the concrete."

I pull myself to my feet and hurry over to Rampir, the Asian who has enlisted me to haul bags of cement up to the second floor. I gather from his breath that he has just finished a breakfast of tinned bean soup and white bread. Since he had no time to heat the beans, he used the bread to eat them straight from the tin, saving himself time and washing-up. The discarded plastic bag and tin sit on top of the construction debris. Unlike him, I brought no breakfast. This body of mine needs only the bare minimum of food to continue hurting. I want to sate my hunger only with the wounds you have inflicted on me.

I bend over to pick up the heavy bag of cement and hear a cracking in my back, a sound which has dogged me for most of the year since the company completed its first project, a seven-storey building. Each floor contains four flats except for the top two floors, which were designed as a luxurious duplex totally unlike the rest of the building. That's no surprise; I later learned that the building's owner intended the duplex as a residence for his son, who was about to get married.

The ground floor comprises a huge empty space that was later rented out as a showroom for imported cars. But whenever groups of visitors and residents in search of the good life get a glimpse of this opulent building that occupies an entire block, they are amazed by how little parking it has. Only a handful of spaces have been set aside for residents, apart from the four spots reserved for the occupant of the luxury duplex that are surrounded by locks and chains to deter prying eyes.

The building's owner never thought to reserve the ground floor for parking or to build a one- or two-storey underground garage. Why should he provide parking for tenants, visitors, or the showroom customers? All he cared about was minimizing his expenses and maximizing his profits. Though he could have made money renting parking spots by the hour, this sort of businessman naturally places his trust only in quick profits. On the other hand, anyone who needs a parking spot can easily find one, since people have taken to parking on vacant lots, the pavement, sometimes even the road. Pedestrians cannot pass one another without stopping, and since the road is now jammed with parked cars, two vehicles headed in opposite directions can no longer pass.

I had come to Oman as the project architect for a shell company that is Omani in name only. Its real owner is the distinguished Kumar Kapoor, that Indian dandy with five rings on his right hand who brought me here purely because he enjoys giving orders to an Arab. I am just one of his many victims. I still remember how surprised I was when I met three architects all working on the same project. At first, I thought it was because the work was of such high quality, but my naive assumption soon gave way to shock when I learned they had become second-class building workers after cheerfully surrendering their passports and their dreams to the dapper Indian. Like me, they had no idea that behind his smile lurked the teeth of a fox that would chew away their lives day after day.

If I was surprised at the extent of Mr. Kapoor's influence here, I was even more amazed at the person who had granted him the use of his name to take possession of this country, plunder its resources, and rob its people. Had generosity induced that person to give away what he had no right to give, or was it a lack of awareness and sense of responsibility that led people down this path of treachery and endless deceit? Overnight, I have been transformed from an architect into a common labourer who hauls bags of cement and listens to his bones cracking.

Houria, are you happy now? Have I already told you that even if I forgave Mr. Kumar for what he has done, it is unlikely I will ever forgive you? Whenever you cross my mind, I grind my teeth, and something in my chest falls and twists in agony, as if it had been bitten. You sent me into exile; you served me up on a platter to this arrogant bastard who knew precisely how to entrap the soul whose serenity you had destroyed.

Don't be surprised that I download your messages and read them. It is just a way to hurt you more. Your knowledge that I have opened and read them is different from my not having received them at all. The first is more hurtful, more painful. So why do I read them? I honestly don't know, maybe to give my long-forgotten laugh a chance to return, even if it's only to jeer at the little anecdotes you are forever sending me.

Four hours of backbreaking labour, during which you are not allowed to stop even for a few minutes to collect your breath or your memories. If you so much as reach your hand out to wipe the sweat from your face, it will come back to you with a torrent of criticism from Sanjay, the foreman. He is exactly like Mr. Kumar, except that Kumar is the dog's head and Sanjay its tail. He wags nonstop when Mr. Kapoor is there and resumes baying at us the moment Kapoor's Mercedes vanishes in a cloud of dust. Nor will you be safe from accusations that you are a lazy slacker who shirks his duties and doesn't earn his wages, most of which you don't deserve anyway.

Speaking of our pay, it is barely enough to live on in this country, of which I know only a single room that I share with three other Arabs and four Asians. It is narrow, no more than three metres by four. Clogged with breathing and stories, it is just big enough to stretch out a foam mattress that is too short, your feet poking out like a child playing hide-and-seek. You rest your head on the meagre belongings that you have stuffed into a piece of broadcloth or stored in a small suitcase. They take up only part of the case, leaving your head to sink into the hollow, as if it were a comfy feather pillow. Like a foetus afraid to depart the womb, you curl up your body so no one can tread on you when he leaves this bottle that they are allowed to call a "workers' room".

Every day this room absorbs our laughter and banter about all the things that happen to us, from which we have learned to be sarcastic. It absorbs the snoring of the workmen when they fling their bodies into their narrow tombs and sleep until the alarm clock lifts its voice, reminding them that if they don't get their act together before the foreman arrives, he may dock their wages. And God help anyone who shows up after the foreman finishes taking attendance. Not only will the latecomer lose his pay for the day; he will get double work and a tongue-lashing whenever the boss catches sight of him. All week long, he will be reminded that he was late, he is sloppy and irresponsible, and he won't be a real man until hunger and fatigue have left their mark on his fat body. The boss will conclude his tirade by pointing out how they have shown us hospitality, though we deserve only contempt. I have no idea what fat body he is referring to, this man so bloated with malevolence. Everyone who works for him is practically featureless, exhausted and emaciated. An observer can distinguish them only by their voices, which pass through the ear like breezes following a rain-swollen cloud preparing to drop its load like a woman in labour.

These voices are raised only at the start of the month, when the workers collect their wages and celebrate with a trip to one of the shops thronged with Asians buying provisions for a whole month, or at least two weeks. On that day, you would not believe you were in an Arab country; everyone who passes you wears his Asian identity on his face. According to my mate Rampir, the city is like this every weekend, and the sight I found so astounding happens every Friday, like clockwork. On Friday, you are bound to meet more than one lost soul that seems only recently to have been parted from its body. For a moment, you might think yourself with all the souls trapped in limbo, the souls of the exhausted and those drowning in pain. They walk as if they have covered no ground, yet they have come from the ends of the earth without ever finding the right door. But you will also meet many faces plump with affluence, who started their meals at the animal's shoulder, its most delicious part, before moving to the nape of its neck, eating until they were full but still not sated. They continued to gorge themselves, gobbling up the heart, the soul and its desires, eating and eating and eating without satisfaction, searching for any vein still pulsing in order to polish it off.

Coming out on Fridays feels like being present on the Day of Judgment, when the dead will congregate. I am not the only one with this impression. I once overheard an Omani tell a friend: "Misery loves company." Rampir finds the situation completely unremarkable. He is used to much bigger crowds in his city, where the poverty of some rivals the wealth of others. Which will triumph and assert its presence? Poverty. Whole families sleep in the street or live in one room, compared to which the cramped room we complain about would be deemed spacious. One room serves as bedroom, living room, and kitchen; the entire neighbourhood shares a single toilet, using it in turns.

In Rampir's city, you can see a temple offering prayers for the neighbouring mosque, which replies with a rousing "Amen." Everyone works to survive and minds his own business. If you pass a wedding procession, you don't pause to watch or offer your congratulations because, quite simply, you weren't invited. Likewise, if you pass a funeral, you don't stop to pay your respects because the dead person is none of your business. A person is preoccupied with his own affairs and those of his family, never thinking of the future.

In Rampir's city, everyone races from dawn to dusk without grumbling or objecting in the belief that it is their fate. Everywhere, people spread out relentlessly, each pursuing himself and his own comfort. There is no rest except for the person who works all the hours God sends without complaining or railing at those who use his heart as a ladder to climb up and pluck the wishes that their own hands cannot reach.

When the sky grew dark, my workmates and I used to sit and share snippets of memory, crumbs that could no longer satisfy our nostalgic cravings. We journeyed with our workmate Ahmad to see his wife, who had given birth in his absence. He had left just as her morning sickness began. Ahmad told us she had asked him not to return because she hated him. But after she gave birth to a boy whom they named Mu'taman—the caretaker, so he would look after his mother—she sent Ahmad a message imploring him to come back because she couldn't adjust to life without him. Ahmad laughs. When he was about to divorce his wife, his mother told him his wife's feelings were nothing but pregnancy cravings. She asked him to delay his return until after the birth, so he did. But the separation had lasted too long; after his wife had given birth, she wanted him back, but he was unable to return.

Then there was Ihsan Akbar, who was constantly telling us about his son, who bore no resemblance to him. Though his son was born two years after Ihsan left, he still celebrated the boy's arrival, distributing sweets and wan smiles to us all. According to Ihsan, in his hometown, people believe the Shaykh's blessings could impregnate a woman as long as her husband had left a pair of trousers with her before he went abroad. This Shaykh always kept an eye on the wives of the men working overseas so they wouldn't fall prey to strangers, visiting them regularly to attend to their needs and checking on them when the nights grew dark. Among the Shaykh's greatest virtues was that some of the children (who might resemble him because he was present when they were in their mother's wombs) may follow in his footsteps and become important people, perhaps even inheriting his knowledge and erudition. I once asked Ihsan: "Do you honestly believe what you're saying?" He answered without hesitation, "Of course." But as he walked away, he wiped his face with his sleeve. Perhaps it was only the sweat of fatigue trickling down his face; I am sure it was not a tear.

We learned to lock our door securely before going to sleep each night, buying ourselves a big padlock with three keys, though I didn't get one. It didn't matter; what use is a key that doesn't open your heart to life? We had become particularly vigilant after the night of terror we lived through six weeks earlier, when we were awoken by the sound of panting above our heads.

Chapter Three

Seeking Refuge

After a year in Oman...

What is warmer than being wrapped in your father's cloak as he takes you to dawn prayers?

After two days living rough, I am starting to think about people who are forced to live outdoors. Now I know what it means to lack a drop of water to slake your thirst or to accept your own stink with helpless resignation, though I once wore only the finest colognes, following my mother's injunction: "Mukhtar must always smell heavenly". I am resigned to my bitter reality, not because I accept God's will and His promise of a reward for those who are patient, but because I have almost no control over my situation.

I follow my footsteps, though I don't know where they are taking me. My phone isn't out of battery yet. Perhaps that's because I keep it turned off, and, to save battery, switch it back on just to check the time, since who knows when I might need it? The phone is clearly fighting for its life, calling on me to revive it before it breathes its last. It bombards me with cries for help: "The battery's empty; please recharge." I pre-empt its entreaties by turning it off before I have to, feeling the intoxication of the victor who's in control of a situation. I contemplate my muscles. Although I used to work out to make them less puny, they never were much to look at. I strike the triumphal pose of a man admiring his bulging biceps. Suddenly, I spot a minaret in the distance and give my feet free rein, ordering them to head there so I can at least get rid of my unpleasant odour and pray.

I stop in my tracks. Did I say "pray"? I can't remember the last time I turned toward Mecca and prayed. I abandoned it after the entreaties I had offered God both day and night did not bring you back. It was as if I had been worshipping God on the edge of a precipice that crumbled and cast me into hellfire. It was not necessarily the hell of the afterlife; there is also a hell on earth, in the hands of the merciless. That was how I managed to forget you and replace my love with hatred. But I did not forget. You remained lodged in my bloodstream like a malignant tumour blocking my circulation. When something hurt me, I would simply pile more blame upon my heart, hoping it would stop and you would die with it.

I walk now, weakness by my side. I don't want to reach toward Heaven as much as I want to smell the earth, to confirm I belong to it and am closely bound to it. I want to celebrate the fact that I am a human, created by God to populate this earth, that I am not superfluous to the needs of the age. My footsteps whisper: retreat, give up; a person like you doesn't deserve to hide from his regrets in the mosque.

My father looks down at me and takes my hand. He doesn't seem angry, like the time he chased me with his cane, when I was only five years old, after the Shaykh at the mosque told him I hadn't shown up for Qur'an classes. That was the Shaykh who flayed us with his cane during every verse, whose blows no one was able to dodge. His cane could reach even the youngest, the shortest, and the furthest away. I don't know how he could reconcile the Qur'an's gentleness with his hardness of heart. When my father told me the Qur'an softens the heart, I would retort that the imam of the mosque had no heart to soften. My father would laugh his ringing laugh, the one to which my mother always turned and smiled with an affectionate shake of her head. He would pull me onto his lap and whisper:

"Mukhtar, you have to memorize the Qur'an so it will intercede for you on Judgment Day."

I would ask: "And when will Judgment Day be?"

"No one knows precisely, but we will all die, and when we do, there in the darkness of our grave, the Qur'an will be your light."

"But I don't want to die, Abi, and I don't want you to die either."

I would like to cry now as I did then, but my father isn't here to put me on his lap and whisper:

"We won't die, Mukhtar. We'll go to paradise, where God will give you anything you want."

"Will he give me a bicycle, Abi?"

"Yes, and a football too."

I stop crying and hug my father tightly, repeating: "Abi, I love you. When is Judgment Day coming?" Then I look at him and ask naively: "What does 'intercede' mean, Abi?"

My father laughs and settles me back onto his lap. "It means wasta, my son, using your influence to help someone. But it's not the kind of wasta people use in everyday life."

He falls silent. My father had always despised wasta, which had made his less-qualified colleague his boss. Out of respect for my father, I keep quiet, since I know he hates this word, but I still don't understand why he wants the Qur'an to help us enter paradise. Maybe it is because the Qur'an will intercede on his behalf, and he is the one who will benefit. I brush these idle thoughts from my mind and inform it—my mind—that my father doesn't like wasta. I close my eyes and fall sleep in my father's lap. He carries me up to bed, tucking me in snugly so the cold cannot harm me.

If only you were here now, Abi, so I could hug you—no, so you could hug me and ease this sorrow dissolving me, so I could melt like ice licked by flames; if only, like ice, I could shrink and vanish. How I wish you would tuck me inside your cloak as you did when you took me to the mosque, the cold assailing my bones after a wild winter night, so I could learn to perform the dawn prayer in a group. If only you would recite the Verses of Refuge over me three times, ending with the Throne Verse, the Verse of the Idolaters, and the Verse of Sincerity, to calm my trembling fingers. They began to shake the day I tried to tell Houria I loved her, though she already knew, feigning indifference and taking it for granted. Ever since that day, I have been unable to control my fingers when they start to shake of their own accord.

The dawn prayer was my favourite, because I could bask in your warmth all the way to the mosque. Never since have I found a warmth to equal that of your cloak. How surprised my mother would be when she came to wake me and I leapt from my bed, asking:

"Has Abi left?"

My mother would smile.

"And would he go without a candle to light the road's darkness? Hurry up, both of you, so you won't miss the prayers."

I approach the mosque, its green minaret topped with a crescent moon that is lit both night and day. It seems the Ottomans were right to place crescents on minarets so as to distinguish mosques from ordinary houses, just as churches have crosses to mark them out. Though it isn't time for prayer, the door of the mosque is ajar, like the doors of heaven.

My mother claims heaven's doors are always open, and if we reach our hand out to God, it will not return empty.

"But He has rejected the hand I've reached out to Him so many times."

"God has a purpose for everything."

"But what is the purpose of our suffering? How does God profit from our misery, our sorrows, and our tears?"

"My son, always remember God. We don't know everything that is unseen. We have to accept our fate and the destiny God has willed for us."

"And am I remembering anyone but Him now?"

My mother stays quiet, holding her tongue so I won't incur God's wrath. She knows I no longer hesitate to speak my mind or care if people accuse me of apostasy and rejecting God's grace. But Mother, what anger could be greater than losing those we love? Though we may see all of life through their eyes, they suddenly drop us like a stray tear.

I say all this through my silence, which lasts so long my mother thinks our call has been cut off. All my conversations with her end this way, in a dialogue that is largely mute. I know what she wants to say, and she knows how I would respond. She remains quiet for long stretches, her breaths echoing down the line, before she calls God's blessings down upon me, asking Him to guide me, open my heart, and bring me back safe and sound so that she can rejoice in me and my children, for whom she has saved up a trove of stories. She hangs up the phone to the sound of a tear teetering on her eyelashes, letting it fall far from me, where my fingers can't reach or comfort it.

The mosque is empty except for the sound of the water I am pouring over myself. I scrub my body fiercely. Not only do I want to wash away its filth and lingering smell; I want my hand to reach my soul, yank it out and plunge it in the water to the point of drowning, over and over again. I smile at my mother, who has taken over the task of scrubbing my mud-caked body, just four years old. My smile widens whenever the soap in my eyes makes me cry, while my mother gently chides me:

"Listen, every time you come home covered in mud, my soap and loofah will be waiting for you!"

I protest, tears leaking through my fingers as I try to rub away the burning soap in my eye, which only turns redder. These days, my eye is still inflamed, but I don't use my fingers to relieve it. My fingers are no longer those childish ones that might have soothed my watering eye. They are coarse now, and if they get near my eye, I will pay a steep price.

"But Mama, all the boys play in the mud."

"Mukhtar isn't like other boys."

And before my mother can finish distracting me from my soapy tears, I hear someone push open the door of the mosque.

Hastily, I stand up and put on the clothes I have already

laid out, keeping my eye on the door to see who is coming. I reach for my phone to check the time; it seems too early for the noon prayer. Is it someone in search of cleanliness, like me, or someone seeking respite from worldly cares? Before I touch my phone, I remember I switched it off to save the battery, and I withdraw my empty hand from my pocket.

The shadow precedes its owner. Long and thin, it stretches out like a towering palm that has been uprooted before offering its trunk to the sun, which playfully hides behind it. I ask myself: What face does this shadow have? What soul shares its length?

Chapter Four

The Café

Several years later, Mukhtar finds work as a waiter

The man who opens his heart to any woman he comes across in sadness and exile, who lets scores of women trample on him, is unfit for love.

Houria

You were a world of wonder to me, of imagination I cannot explain, magic that forged marvels, leaving me no chance to close my eyes in case I missed the tiniest detail. Give me your hand and let the moments go where they will, for there is one moment that will always unite us. I know I am not a summer cloud or a passing dream, and that is enough. I know I am the only woman whom you have loved as if she were the last woman in creation; I know no other woman shares any part of your heart, and that is enough.

I want you to sing me to sleep; I want to drift off to your voice as I giggle without telling you the reason—that you have a tin ear.

My dearest, I have grown ashamed of my voice, which is infused with sadness, ashamed of wishing I could speak to you of joy and dreams and white nights concealed behind the darkness. But my voice rebels. I can no longer control it, imprisoning it in a bottle that I throw into the sea, where a storm may shatter it beyond repair. I cannot hide from you that I have started to leave my windows open before I go to sleep for fear my voice will kill me, although once I forgot and closed them. My voice rose around me, filling the air of my room until I was about to suffocate. Louder, louder, louder, don't cover your ears with your hands, please; I am afraid of what will happen to your hands when my voice assaults them and they cannot ward it off.

You are faithless. Like all men, you forget quickly, living as if love hadn't brought you into the world of manhood quickly, and perhaps too soon. You men fill your time with friends and women, but none of you dares turn around to see the woman he left behind, her lifeless, worn-out body like a piece of uncut cloth, after she had allowed herself to be measured for the heart of a man she swore had escaped heaven to sleep on her breast.

You are a liar. You have never loved; you won't get down on your hands and knees even to make the face of your beloved bloom with jasmine. Not only are you faithless; you are a liar and a coward as well, who ran away before I could tell you that one day, I would love you as if you were the last man the earth sired before it died and the sea swallowed it.

What a fool I am! I've told myself before: the man who opens his heart to any woman he happens upon in sadness and exile is unfit for love. So I berate myself as I try to stop my heart from compounding its error. But my heart knows I am lying. It ignores me and repeats: "I love him so much that I cannot live without him. Even if he looks at another woman, she will be nothing but a passing whim."

Every night, I imagine you with another woman, who falls asleep to your voice and wakes to your face. I swear to myself that these are not just the delusions of a forsaken woman, but actual facts. I picture your heart flinging open its doors to any woman who comes in search of love; I see a thousand women surge through your bloodstream each night.

That's enough nonsense, I shout at myself; pull yourself together and leave him to the floozies and the troublemakers. You are an idiot to run after him like this. You love him so much—I know—though he does not deserve it. But I always fail to convince myself. I know I am lying, I know myself when I lie. I learned how to lie when I was still at school, only thirteen years old, and fibbed to explain why I had missed two days of class. I claimed I had been ill, but it wasn't true; I had only had my first period. Embarrassed and confused, I hid from my father and everyone else until your mother came to check on me. I cried in her arms until she calmed me down by telling me everything was fine, and having periods just meant I was more beautiful and grown-up.

These days, I hide my hands behind my back to convince everyone of my honesty; I no longer cross my arms defensively or wave them about to distract others from what I am saying. Now, I stare directly into my eyes instead of letting them wander over their surroundings. I cannot stand it, Mukhtar, I will die if you so much as touch another woman; my heart will stop. These miserable thoughts scar my soul, and I spend my evenings weeping, praying only for your return.

I wanted to tell you something that's too important to wait. I have searched high and low for my voice, but I cannot find it. I rifled through your old gifts, I looked in my overflowing drawers, my old suitcases stored on top of the wardrobe, underneath the cold cushions, and behind the last year that I spent apart from you, but I could not find it. My voice is convinced there is no point in sending messages that don't reach you, so it has chosen to stay silent and remain aloof, because it knows I can only chatter about you and to you. My body is dripping with sweat. I am listless and my heart will not be still. Have I been dreaming? I don't know. I want to sleep now more than ever. I will sleep.

I know I was wrong, and I know God is all-forgiving, all-merciful. But who are you to look down on the laws of God and nature? Why can't you forgive a mistake I have paid for with years of my life, lost one after another, a mistake for which you too have sacrificed years? If I hadn't carried you in my heart all my life, I would be a married woman by now, enjoying the warmth of a man and the mischief of a child, going to bed before ten p.m. and waking when the birds peck at my window, fixing sandwiches and laughter and quick kisses for my husband and children before waving them goodbye as they depart with their dreams on their backs or in their hands.

But I have staked my life on waiting, on the never-ending minutes and seconds that press down on my eyes and enter them every time I blink. I never thought that my body would carry a child who was not yours, who did not look like you or have your eye colour or affectionate touch. I never imagined I would not see him run toward you to pick him up and toss him in the air as he squealed with delight, secure in the knowledge his father would never drop him.

Do you know the most painful part? I will never hear him call you "Baba." I won't hear you laugh as you lie on your back and he clambers over you mischievously. You won't lead him by the hand wherever you go; he won't grow up by your side where you can support him when adolescence overtakes him. We won't draw his dreams or write his days together; you won't choose his name, and I won't give him the name you wanted for him. It's not as bad as you think—it's worse.

Love is a marvellous thing. It comes when we least expect it and takes our hearts, then departs, leaving our bodies spent, unable to live. Time marches over them and leaves its mark—wrinkles shallow or deep according to the events that crossed our once-smooth skin; scars on hidden parts of the body, or perhaps in places that are visible; dark circles under our eyes and sometimes above them; forced smiles; and not a single tear, since tears are for the affluent, while we must swallow ours until we choke.

And now here I am, running down the same streets that watched as you pursued me, seeking the favour of a woman who smiled with conceit whenever she looked in the mirror. Swaying coquettishly, she blew a kiss to that angelic face, overflowing with femininity, and it gazed rapturously back at her, sure that only she had been endowed with such an abundance of charm. You did not reproach me on that day, or scold me or raise your voice. You simply whispered, as if addressing the heavens:

"You don't realize you are killing me, but I won't forget to tell God that I love you." And you left.

As if your whisper had pierced the sky and bounced back, striking me dead on the spot, my love for you has grown from that day onwards until I can no longer bear it. I have begun reciting your spell, hoping it will bounce back and cut you down:

"You don't realize you are killing me, but I won't forget to tell God that I love you."

However, my voice is too feeble to reach the sky; it will not even leave my chest. I will die alone, without your palm reaching for my forehead to brush away the fear and the absence, though they are indelible.

Mukhtar

One message after another, with no connection between them except that you sent them. Some are passionate, some angry, and others remorseful or delusional. Sometimes you are the victim, sometimes the criminal. You choose whether to stay away or return, depending on your whims and mood. I don't know when you are going to give up and forget me. How many messages have you sent— hundreds, thousands? I am no longer sure of the exact number, and it doesn't matter. They are just numbers that mean nothing when the messages are cold, filled only with star-crossed memories. I raise my unsteady fingers to delete them, sending them to join their sisters who have met the same fate. The esteemed Mr. Facebook warns me:

"Once you delete your copy of this conversation, it cannot be undone."

I want to tell the worthy gentleman that I have no plans to undelete them, but he isn't fond of chatting, so I repeat:

"Delete chat."

My days come and go, revolving to the rhythm of the circle that spins on my screen as it erases our conversation. I wonder whether Amjad has tried to cosy up to you. Have you been seduced by the money you didn't find with me? That oaf Amjad with his pot belly and his sunken eyes behind their eternally puffy lids? Amjad, who owns everything but still believes he has nothing? Have you thought seriously of marrying him, showing off by riding in his new car or lying beside the swimming pool in the garden of his big house? How often have I imagined your fingers caressing his face? How often did his arms map the limits of your kingdom? Have you dreamt of kissing him? Aren't you disgusted by how he spits when he talks? Have your dreams expanded to bearing his child, even as you hope fervently that it will look like you, not him? Would you still love him if he turned out to be a replica of his obese father?

I put my head in my hands. Damn your messages—they take me to you, scorched as I am by my sarcasm and jealousy. I delete them from my phone, but they invade my soul. You know how to suck the life from my veins without mercy; just as I am about to forget, you show up, and whenever I smile, you rebel, joining me in my exile and longing, forcing me to share your fear, pain, and tears. Neither of us has forgotten, not because we can't, but because we don't want to.

Hajj Salih pulls me from the vortex of my thoughts.

"Muhammad Mukhtar, take the customer's order."

I put down my phone and run toward the deep blue car with the yellow license plate numbered 44, looking to see what model it is. It's a Porsche Cayenne. Oh my God! How many lifetimes would I need to buy a car like this? "In your dreams!" I jeer at myself. Apparently it belongs to a rich person, one of those so wealthy they have no idea what to do with their money, or who go into debt to pretend they are rich. Anyway, the car's model isn't important. Right now, I need to show the customary appreciation and respect for the gentleman lounging behind the wheel of this luxury car. When I reach the car, he opens his window, and the air conditioning wafts over me. It's as if a window from paradise has opened onto the hell of Muscat's unbearable summer. I paste a smile on my face, but before I can take his order, his voice comes to me, filled with courtesy:

"Lemon with mint, please, and lots of ice." I trade my false smile for one thanking him for his courtesy, as my voice leaps to fill his order:

"One minute."

I run inside, my inner voice asking: "Hey you! Will it really only be one minute?" But it's okay, I doubt it will make much difference, since time doesn't matter to those living in paradise. I hastily prepare the juice, keeping one eye on the clock as the seconds race ahead of me. I add plenty of ice to give the polite young man what he deserves. I can see now that he isn't one of the nouveaux rich. They never miss the chance to mock their social inferiors, whereas those who come from old money always, with rare exceptions, have good manners.

"Hurry up, Mukhtar! The customer's waiting."

Hajj Salih is always interrupting my train of thought. I run to the car and hand the customer the juice before taking his payment and returning, as Hajj Salih fingers the white prayer beads he brought back from Mecca. This good-hearted man makes the pilgrimage almost every year. If, for some reason, he misses a year, he does not fail to go the following one. So I was told by the employees who started working here before me. Inside Hajj Salih, there is a veritable home for emigres, not just a heart weakened by his chronic anaemia. A self-made man who worked as a waiter when he first came to Oman, he now owns his own cafe after ten years of labouring night and day and a great deal of penny-pinching for himself and his family, who never complained or threw their poverty back in his face and abandoned him.

"The woman is the pillar of the house."

That's what Hajj Salih is always saying. Had his wife not secretly saved any money left over after paying for their food, he could not have opened this cafe. When he despaired of ever owning his own cafe, she surprised him with the funds for the shortfall. When he asked her where it had come from, she claimed to have set aside money for a rainy day. In fact, she had sold her wedding ring behind his back and pretended to have lost it.

"No woman is the equal of Hajja Halima."

Hajj Salih smiles as he leans back in his rosewood chair, carved with intricate, regular designs that portray nothing in particular.

Four young Arab men work in Hajj Salih's cafe alongside two Asians who have learned the art of preparing juice in an astonishing way. We share a single flat on the third floor of the building where the cafe is located, in a busy commercial district, separated from it by only two floors. We start work at ten in the morning and finish at midnight, with one day off a week to do what we like and go where we want. Unfortunately, our days off don't coincide; each of us gets a different day. So we recently agreed, with Hajj Salih's approval, to take our holiday in pairs so we could enjoy it.

Under the rota we had established, we began at 10 a.m., preparing the juices we could make in advance. For juices such as orange and lemon, that had to be made to order lest they spoil, we cut the fruit up beforehand so customers would not have to wait. We also agreed that one of us would stay to make lunch and drew up a rota for that. Hajj Salih has opened a new branch, far from the capital Muscat, and from what we hear, two of us will take charge of it. The branch where we now work will have to manage with just four employees. Right now, there are six of us, and we don't have a moment to spare, so how will we operate with only four?

"If it's too hard for you, I'll hire more staff."

So Hajj Salih cut us off before we could ask him or reveal our thoughts. Either our faces gave us away or he could see right through us.

Ten months passed serenely, disturbed only by longing and my mother's voice, which I couldn't pick up and wrap around me whenever the cold assaulted me, and by your relentless messages. Sometimes you are apologetic and sometimes accusatory. Sometimes you express your love and other times you hurl your angry words into your long messages. If you knew—if only you knew—how days go by for the emigre, the one cast out from the grace of nations. His only sin was your two eyes, which have made a home in his soul since you were seven years old, when neither of you knew the first thing about love. As your eyes grew, his heart grew with them, but your soul and your desires did not. His love was equal to his hurt, and his hurt equalled the difficulty of forgiving.

During those ten months, I did not complain of my humiliation, my weakness, or my powerlessness. Who am I, anyway, that life should make me laugh and grant me the rest I deserve? I know life only as a viper that bides its time, waiting for the moment to inject its venom.

Then a dispute broke out between Hajj Salih and his Omani partner, in whose name the business was registered. They had agreed that Hajj Salih would give the owner a reasonable sum each month, in return for which the owner need do nothing. But apparently Hajj Salih's success and the fact that he was opening new branches had introduced a new partner—greed—which would only be satisfied when it had spoiled everything. The Omani partner demanded half the profits, though he was not contributing a single riyal. If Hajj

Salih did not agree, his only choice would be to return to his country, leaving behind his youth and his dreams for the foreigner to enjoy. Pardon me, I mean the rightful owner, the Omani citizen, since we—myself, Hajj Salih, and everyone working for him—are the foreigners here.

Chapter Five

The Construction Site

Mukhtar's second year in Oman

As we await a loved one who does not come, our eyes remain open after death.

There were three of them, speaking in whispers, water dripping from their bodies as if they had emerged from the sea. And in fact, they had just stepped out of its waters after a rubber raft dumped them on the shore, its owner pocketing his exorbitant fee and abandoning them to their uncertain fate. They had had the misfortune of ending up with us, desperate men who knew nothing of life but a cold wooden room, three metres by four, that had never seen or smelled paint.

We awoke that night with terror in our midst. Each of us left his bed and hid beside his neighbour. That night, we learned how fortunate we were to share this room; although we were unrelated, it had brought us together like brothers. The men asked us only to provide them shelter and relieve the hardships of their journey with some sleep and a little food. They communicated mostly with signs, occasionally uttering a few words in Arabic like "Muslim", "food", or "sleep", which they appeared to have memorized in advance. Since we felt sorry for them, our fear began to yield to compassion. We could see ourselves in them; they were foreigners, like us, though we possessed more than they did.

As we compared notes with the newcomers, we realized we were all miserable wretches to whom life had been unfair. All of us were the offspring of poverty, which had sired us before abandoning us to hunger, loss, winding roads and wasted years, an unjust father who demanded our fidelity with no assurance of a brighter future. My roommates and I gave each other sidelong looks, but Rampir, who had known—and lost—love in his youth, was the first to extend a hand to them. He searched out any food he could find to silence the cries of their bellies, which were baying like starving wolves.

It is said wolves howl with joy when they are hungry because they know they will soon be full, but when they are full, they howl mournfully because they know hunger is not far behind. Even wolves know instinctively that the world keeps on turning, or, as the proverb says, "Nothing stays the same". So although we were both reluctant and terrified, especially after watching the men devour their food, we decided to help Rampir welcome the men.

The guests of darkness finished eating. Tall and fair-skinned, the three men wore ordinary clothing that didn't reveal where they were from. All three had thick, smooth black hair that hung to their shoulders. I touched my own hair. My receding hairline had left a space where the noon sun revelled and sweat ran freely down my face. When the visitors were nearly asleep, we were startled to hear feet kicking in the unlocked door and a light that blinded us rather than illuminating the darkness. After our eyes had adjusted to the sudden glare, we found ourselves surrounded by policemen with pistols and long black batons, who hauled us all off to the police station.

It was a long night, with no sleep and no wages the following day. God knows how long we would have stayed in gaol if our boss hadn't brought our confiscated ID cards. I could have seized the chance to save myself from this hellhole and expose the conspiracy I had been the victim of, but I was afraid of ending up like these migrants. They would languish in prison until being deported to their home countries as if they had never left them, with nothing to show for their journey but wasted money, vanished dreams, and huge, inestimable losses. So I swallowed my misery and went along with whatever Kumar Kapur said, as his dogsbody Sanjay barked beside him.

That night passed, yet it seemed it would never end. The next day, we were forced to work late to compensate for the morning we had spent at the police station. Though we had not slept and did a double shift, working through our mealtimes to complete the never-ending work, the decision came down, as if to torture us, that we would be fined a day's wages as punishment for welcoming the infiltrators. We held our tongues, though some of us glared at Rampir, because he had been the first to help them. But Rampir just retreated to his bed and sat there crying.

I went over to him and touched his shoulder gently, but he only hunched over more. I said consolingly:

"I appreciate what you did, my friend; you showed compassion. Don't worry, everything will be all right."

But Rampir just said: "Maybe one of them has a sweetheart waiting for him to bring her dowry so he can gain her father's approval. Now he'll have to break off their engagement. Perhaps one has a sick mother and used her medication money to buy his passage on a rubber dinghy that could have sent him to his death instead of to prison or his dreams."

"But Rampir, they were wrong; we all know it. No country lets people infiltrate its borders like this. We're getting emotional here, but the police are protecting the security of their country."

"Do you think I'm blaming the police for doing their jobs? I'm not; I'm just thinking about those men. How are they different from us? We managed to get here because we had nice passports with colour photos of us smiling big phony smiles, but this country received us like slave labourers, tearing the smiles off our faces the moment we arrived. Are we any better off than these men? Who says they weren't also dreaming of passports with doctored colour photos that would help them reach their heart's desire—work visas to secure their future? They were lured here just like us, on their own, without any family, children, or sweethearts waiting for them."

I lift my hand from his shoulder to lighten his load, but he huddles up further, perhaps to keep warm. Looking for something to distract myself, I glance over at our companions. Each has retreated to a corner to savour his misery alone, undisturbed by the others. I abandon myself to my bed and press my tears into my pillow, searching for a face to lull me to sleep without chattering, but my insomnia won't let anyone join me. This night is like that one long ago, when I lay awake till dawn and vomited from exhaustion.

Tonight, too, I could not sleep. I decided to go outside for some fresh air to escape the cramped, suffocating room. The calm outside drowned out the breaths of the dreaming workers inside. Only a few voices intruded in an effort to dominate the utter silence and the darkness that was gradually overtaking the sleeping night, whose moon had retired early. The voices did not concern me; they were probably just irksome passers-by. I switched on my phone to light my path and headed away from the building site and our room with its wooden walls and lightweight aluminium roof, easy to dismantle and transport to a new site.

This cold roof shows us no mercy in winter. It is not content merely to lash our bodies with cold draughts, but conspires with every drop of the rain we would normally welcome, turning us into fugitives who huddle together to escape it as it joins the roof in mocking us. The more the rain pours down, the louder the roof cackles and the more buckets we place to catch the raindrops defying the roof's feeble efforts at resistance.

Last winter was particularly harsh. Not only was it cold, but it rained so much that the floor of our room was transformed into a sandbar by runoff from the unfinished building, whose fragile foundations we had not yet reinforced. I remember how we awoke one morning to find muddy water streaming beneath us, forcing us to replace our mattresses later on. As we repaired our room, how we rejoiced when we found a tiny plant pushing its way up through the muddy floor.

We decided to nurture the plant and see what it would become. Never mind that it took up floor space; at least it wouldn't deprive us of oxygen, since it consumed the carbon dioxide we exhaled. In short, it was just another of the abundance of blessings here, and we were crestfallen when it wilted after a few days, although we had watered it. In all likelihood, we had drowned it, since every worker who passed by splashed it with his water bottle so as to feel his importance in the life of this fragile seedling. Or perhaps it couldn't bear life in our room, which was ill-prepared for a new guest.

As it was, the inhabitants could barely thread their way through the bodies slumbering in exhaustion. Rarely could one of us pass without treading on one of his companions and adding to their misery as it slept peacefully inside their bodies. What losers we were, searching for crumbs of meaning in a plant we hoped would blossom one day into a jasmine bush or a bitter orange tree! It might have come from a seed we had once discarded. Only Ihsan Akbar said: "Maybe it will be an orange tree with delicious fruit. Why not? True, we've never shared an orange and thrown away the pips, but God has power over everything."

"Just like his wife bore him a son two years after he left home," Ihsan's workmates mocked him behind his back, so he would not overhear.

I steal a glance at my phone. The clock has jumped forward half an hour; it's almost three in the morning. I must have walked a long way, since I can no longer see our room. I retrace my steps, hoping to get some rest before handing my body back to the foreman so he can continue to violate my rights as well as those of everyone else who works for him. I notice that the strange noise at the construction site is still going on, and I head for the room, where all the workers are still as dead to the world as when I left. The grinding labour that extracts its due from them during the day harvests them by night, when they drop to the ground motionless, the only sign of life the heavy rise and fall of their chests. Usually nobody wakes up until his bladder is about to burst, when he stumbles outside with bleary eyes; if his feet didn't know the way, he would crash into every last body littering the floor.

Curious to discover the source of the noise, I put my phone on silent. Approaching the building, I try to peer inside. It isn't totally dark. Small flashlights are roving around, held by men I have never seen before. They are hauling bags of cement and electrical cables back and forth. I hear a voice outside ordering them to hurry up before any workers wake up and notice they're there. The voice sounds familiar, but in the darkness, I can't see who it is.

I hear a car leave—I can't tell what model—and return to my room. Anyway, it's none of my business. There seems to have been a robbery that will be discovered in the morning, but I have no need to court trouble. As for my roommates, they are sunk in their dreams. Stumbling toward my empty bed, I bump into Ajay, who rolls over just as I step across him. But for the grace of God, I would have fallen on him. I look like a circus performer teetering on a high wire before he falls, shattering his bones and dreams all at once.

I allow the thought of Ajay to enter my troubled mind: skinny Ajay, tossing and turning in his sleep. He is the only workmate I can't look at directly. His deep green eyes are pools of magic, mystery, and sadness. Ajay once told me he had allowed his fiancée to marry another man after that thief of dreams had made off with her in a luxury car. She now had two children, who neither looked like Ajay nor were his offspring. Though her smile was still as radiant as the moon, her amber eyes had darkened to the colour of bitter coffee. Ajay spent his evenings picturing his beloved in the arms of the man who had bought her. Whether she had sold herself to him willingly or under duress, as she claimed, was not important, since the result was the same. However, those evenings were not as painful as the ones in which Ajay mourned his mother. When she died, he hadn't been allowed to travel for a final look at her cherished body before the funeral pyre consumed her soft flesh and her ashes were scattered over the river.

In his childhood, how often he had plunged into that river to swim, bathe, or play with his friends, their bodies smeared with mud and colourful powders! How could he surrender to its arms again after it had carried away his mother's ashes? Would the river remember his tawny body that once dived into its waters during the festival of Holi, which had coloured it like the rainbow after a storm? Ajay once told me: "How can I bear to go back when I don't know what tree has grown from my mother's ashes or what soul they have nourished? In our country, the person closest to the mother's heart scatters her ashes. As her only son, I should have done it, but since I wasn't there, someone else had to. The neighbours said it was the temple priest.

"My mother fixed her eyes on the heavens and waited for me to descend, declaring that the gods would send me to her in a passing cloud. She asked them not to close her eyes if she died before I got there, in case something pressing had delayed my response to her deathbed summons. She waited for me so she could go to her final rest in peace, convinced I would come so she could gaze on me one final time, even from the heart of her funeral pyre.

"Even if I could forget my mother, whose ashes the river took before I could follow to see where they washed up, how could I forget my father? The river flood swept him away before depositing its silt on our small piece of land, as if in apology for taking its sole caretaker. Even our little plot is waiting for me, waiting for the sweat I used to spread on its soil or wash off in the river. But in the end, I let it down; I abandoned it and ran away like the ungrateful child and coward I am."

Ajay opens his eyes while I am still standing there like someone who longs to store up even more pain in his memory. He studies me, his green eyes like a deep river that knows you are going to drown in it, and surprises me by asking:

"Haven't you gone to sleep yet?"

I suddenly remember what I have just seen and worry that if I tell him the truth, I will expose myself to accusations or worse. I reply casually: "Yes, but I had to use the toilet." All of us share the bathroom beside our room, waiting for up to an hour for a few minutes of peace and quiet. If someone gets bored or tired and takes a break, he has to go to the back of the queue or the others will eat him alive. We are all used to this system and no longer mind the wait. The alternative is showering in a bucket of cold water in front of everyone, covered only by your underwear, or doing your business outdoors, seeking a private corner that is out of sight. But who cares if people witness our bodily excretions? It is bad enough that our injured souls are visible to the entire world.

Chapter Six

The Date Farm

After the construction site

Sometimes we need to lie a bit in order to survive, when truthfulness is just a dry crust that satisfies neither body nor soul.

From behind his long, thin shadow appears an equally gaunt Asian carrying an empty water bucket and long broom. Not looking at me, he begins to pray, performing two prostrations before starting to sweep the mosque courtyard. I feel naked before him, though I am wearing my underclothes.

"You will pray now", I command my soul, convinced it must obey me. For the first time, the Devil does not come and tell me not to pray or remind me that the One who deprived me of my beloved does not deserve my thanks. So it seems to be true: devils don't enter mosques. I begin to approach God, prostrating myself once, twice, and then three, four times. I lose track of my prostrations and the number of prayers and Qur'anic verses I have recited as I beg God to forgive me, show me mercy and rescue me from my predicament. Whether from piety or pain, I unburden my sadness, prostrating myself for so long that the Asian touches my shoulder with concern, pulling me from my reunion with God.

"Are you all right?"

I raise my head and finish praying, as he squats beside me like a dog faithfully guarding his sleeping master.

"As-salamu alaykum."

His voice drops onto me, peaceful and cool as a gentle rain, seeping through my pores into my soul.

"I was praying", I respond, then fall silent. I don't lift my eyes from where I've been praying; I am afraid my weakness will get the better of me, and I will revert to exhaustion, despair, and alienation, or that the world will rob me of the faith I have just begun to reclaim.

"You seem to be deeply devout. I've rarely seen anyone concentrate so hard on their prayers. You were prostrate for so long I thought you might have died."

"Do I look devout?"

"'On their faces, they bear the marks of their prostrations,'" he said, smiling as he recited the verse, a simple worker cleaning the mosque who knew more of the Qur'an than I did.

Am I really devout? I don't think so. Shaykh Yassin always said the opposite. God rest your soul, Shaykh Yassin, I think you would have threatened this skinny Asian with your cane for calling me devout or bashed him on the head to bring him back to his senses and shut him up.

My thoughts carried me far away. I cannot say whether it was the memories flooding through my mind or those lodged within it that disturbed my peace of mind. I journeyed to my country. I kissed my mother and flung myself into my father's arms. I recited great chunks of the Qur'an in front of Shaykh Yassin. I fought with Amjad and won. I proposed marriage to Houria, and after she accepted with delight, we went on an outing and ate grilled corn and ice cream.

"You're looking for work, right?" the man asked with the smile of an expert who had plucked out my soul, cross-examined it, then put it back, well-pleased and well-pleasing. I froze and began trembling again. So quickly, God? I wasn't prepared for your answer yet; I hadn't thought about it or even finished praying. I was still searching for a window to You, so how did You get here first?

"I can help you."

Please, be quiet for a moment. I haven't trained my tongue to answer quickly; I can't take in what you're saying. Did God send you as an angel in human form? I touch my fingers. Yes, I am still alive; my shaking limbs confirm it.

"Yes."

That word was all I needed for him to take my hand and help me to my feet. Before I could remember the clothes I had left by the washbasin, he scooped them up along with my other belongings and led me outside the mosque. I did not bother to ask where we were going, what kind of work he had, his name or position or anything else.

"My name is Taj al-Islam. I work over there on that farm, where I live in a small room. When the trees are being irrigated, I come here and give the mosque a quick clean. The locals pay me whatever they can, without any contract or conditions. The owner of the farm has been trying to find someone to help me during harvest season, when the farm needs more hands to relieve it of its burden of many months."

"But...."

"Don't worry, I'll teach you everything. But don't tell the owner you have no experience. I'll say you were working on a farm, but the boss didn't pay you, so you had to find another job to keep from starving."

"But...."

"If I tell him the truth, he won't hire you."

He added with a sigh: "Sometimes, we need to tell a few lies to survive, when truthfulness is just a dry crust that satisfies neither body or soul. We lie so we won't die of hunger. I used to be like you; I didn't know a thing, but I learned. If you hadn't seemed like an upright man, I wouldn't have helped you."

My voice faltering, I asked him: "Do you really think I'm upright?"

"Either upright or penitent. Whichever it is, I have to help you, or I'll be no better than the Devil."

We entered the farm, a former paradise that appeared to have been struck by a celestial calamity. The landscape was ravaged. All that remained were a few trees, clearly planted recently to cover up death's march across the land, and a line of palms that encircled the farm like a bracelet or cordon ready to pounce on any intruders. The palms had withstood the drought that had gnawed away all the adjoining trees. Noticing my surprise, Taj al-Islam spoke before I could ask:

"Like all the farms around here, this farm was planted with every kind of tree and crop, but the drought killed everything. Only a few farms survived, the ones built near the reservoirs that store rainwater and keep it from running out to sea. That is how some lands dried up and others took over the water supplies. These farms are like humans—the big devour the small. But despite the drought, these palms have continued to grow, sinking their roots deeper into the ground as if to say: 'I will not abandon my land to strangers.'

"Oh yes, I forgot to tell you that many of these farms have been sold off. One day, the villagers woke to find that foreigners were offering astronomical prices, sums beyond their wildest dreams. The sky seemed to be raining gold, and everyone reached out for some. When the villagers finally realized what was happening, they no longer owned any land. Only a handful understood the situation and did not succumb to the temptations they were offered. Among them was the owner of this farm. He spends more on it than he earns, but he says this land is his life, and he would die if he lost it."

"What's odd is that these lands were supposedly going to be developed for tourism, but now they lie fallow, and no one is interested in them. They have suddenly lost their value and their share prices have dropped so low that no one will buy them. Nobody knows what happened. It's said that the partners had a disagreement or there was a funding shortfall. The cynical claim that certain powerful people in the country had their eye on the lands and the profits from the tourist development, and decided only they would benefit from them, so that's what happened. But they didn't lift a finger, so the project ground to a halt. As a result, no one has benefitted—neither foreigners nor locals. Agricultural lands have become barren: the buildings are unfinished; the walls are in ruins; and the billboard was eaten away by the elements. It's like the saying: 'He shows no mercy, and he prevents God's mercy from descending to His servant.'"

Taj al-Islam's generosity toward me made me suspect his intentions. Why should he help a stranger of whom he knew nothing but how he prayed? Later on, though, Taj told me that my prayers had been enough to judge my character, since only the pure of heart could pray as I had.

And so the first day passed quickly, between Taj al-Islam's stories about this quiet village and a lunch of spicy Indian food. My stomach, empty for two days, was not used to the food, and I had diarrhoea till the following day. In the evening, I threw my tired bones onto Taj al-Islam's bed, which felt luxurious after two nights sleeping in the shade of a tree or behind a rock, and gave myself over to a dreamless sleep. Even dreams have no appetite for the weak and rejected, those cast out from life's grace. And before the day began to yawn and shoot the arrow of its sun into night's quiver, Taj al-Islam shook me awake to announce that the boss had come to discuss my duties here. I would lie about my expertise so Taj al-Islam could start to teach me the work, and Am Sulayman, the farm's owner, could start to commend my efforts, which I thought were no better than the patched rags of a dervish.

Am Sulayman was a kindly man. When I saw his grandchildren cluster around him as if searching for warmth, I remembered how my father used to put me on his shoulders and fly with me as I closed my eyes and stretched out my arms, feeling wrapped in the security of the whole world. Both Am Sulayman and my father had hearts of light. They seemed to have been created in paradise before descending to take their rightful places on earth, where they perfumed the hearts of everyone around them.

Each morning, Am Sulayman came to the farm with pots of tea and coffee and enough breakfast for several people. He brought enough to feed me, Taj al-Islam, and any chance guests—for which he would be rewarded in the Hereafter—and threw the leftovers to every single animal. Birds flocked to the breadcrumbs he scattered, and even the ants had their share. I used to watch armies of ants march over Am Sulayman as he sat motionless so they would not flee and abandon their winter provisions to the summer's mouth. This man deserved his name, for like the Prophet Sulayman, he had been endowed with the speech of birds and granted dominion over the universe.

Chapter Seven

The Café

Mukhtar meets Abdallah from Yemen

We do not forget, not because we cannot, but because we will not.

Mukhtar

A year ago, I killed a child. He was throwing something at me,
I'm not sure what, but it fell beside him, far from me. Maybe it was
something light: a piece of paper, a flower perhaps, or one of those
small plastic toys you can't buy for children under three in case they
choke on them. I really don't know. Though the thing didn't land far
from him, I was still confused and fearful. I knew that if that child
grew up, he would kill me. His wide eyes, the yellow of fresh Sidr
honey, revealed it. The looks he threw in my direction swore to it.
I am no expert in the language of the eyes, but you could read this
child's eyes from the very first glance.

I killed him, yes, I admit it; I had no choice. He was singing a
song I knew, one I used to hear in the church beside our home when
someone died. I can hear that song now, but there is no church next
to the courthouse and the prisoners haven't smuggled me news of
anyone's death. I cover my mouth and swallow hard. God loves me;
surely He will forgive me. He doesn't wish for me to die today; at
least I don't think he does.

The child is still lying in wait for me. So he has not died; he was
only pretending so they would execute me. What a little devil, sitting
innocently on the judge's bench holding something in his hand:
a toy, a flower or a bit of paper shaped like an airplane, no, like a
sailboat perhaps. He looks at me with disinterest before returning
to his toy as if I'm not there. He must think I don't deserve a second
look, or perhaps he is sure I'm as good as dead. The judge raises his
voice, oblivious to the child playing on his bench, whom I'm sure has

bribed the judge to sentence me to death.

"In view of the lack of conclusive evidence, and although the accused has confessed to his crime—perhaps for mental reasons, as the defence counsel is claiming, based on reports from the Hospital for the Mentally Ill—we find the defendant innocent of the charges against him. We further find that he is entitled to counter-sue the victim's family for material and moral damages because of the psychological harm this accusation has brought to him and his reputation. The court is adjourned."

Two police officers led me from the dock where I'd been placed with my hands bound. The child was no longer at his place on the bench. His toy had flown into the sky, taking him with it. He did not wave to me, but smiled and sang the same irritating song that was echoing in the courtroom. I pulled my hands away from the policemen and covered my mouth. Thinking I was trying to escape, one of the policemen raised his pistol and fired at me.

I woke up singing, music tumbling from my lips as I opened my eyes, my body soaked with sweat as if I'd just emerged from a torrential downpour. I reached out and touched my knee. It felt sticky; apparently the bullet had struck it. I touched the viscous liquid and raised my hand to see its colour. It wasn't the colour of blood; my hand wasn't damp, and no warm liquid dribbled through my fingers. Have I lost my blood, or has it been dried up by fear? Have I become as bloodless as all the other exiles here, or is this just a dream, as usual? It's clear I'm dreaming.

It seems I will never escape the shadow of Abdullah, whom I'd known as Abu Bakr since first meeting him during his shift at the Yemeni restaurant next to the shop where I worked. Abdullah and I shared a flat with four other men, two of whom worked with me and two with him. Abdullah had come to Oman for medical treatment after being injured. He left the hospital with graver wounds after learning he had lost his daughter and wife, who was seven months pregnant with their son Bakr. His wife and unborn child had died in the bombing that destroyed their home. After Abdullah regained consciousness, he was sure it was his wife and daughter Yara whom he had imagined during his coma. He used to sing to Yara each morning as he drove the taxi he had bought after ten years in exile selling coffee, mixed nuts, folk remedies, and some of his health, youth, and dignity in what he still calls a "brotherly" Arab country. Abdullah and his passengers would croon along to the words of Fairouz:

Yara, the one with the golden locks

A lifetime swings in them...

But that lifetime was cut short, before the swing could bring Yara back, when she ran joyfully toward the bombs falling on her home as she shouted:

"Abi, the sky is raining stars!"

Abdullah couldn't tell his daughter that the falling things were not stars, but vicious predators. Nor did he manage to reach Yara and his wife before the savage stars flattened them to the ground. He fell, too, after the bomb blast had flung him in the air. He closed his eyes, expecting to open them on the sight of Yara collecting the stars so they could bloom like flowers. But when he awoke, she was asleep far away, in a city where the stars always shine and flowers never wilt. His seventy-year-old father was the next to die. The old man had borne the death of his wife—the mother of his children—alone, never complaining of his weakness, fatigue, and loneliness. But he could not endure the sight of little Yara torn apart, the child who used to wake each morning and bring him candy as she asked in her childish voice:

"Which hand, jaddi?"

How delighted she would be when he guessed wrong, since she knew that she alone would enjoy the candy after generously insisting he taste some. She didn't realize the candy was bigger than her small hands and her grandfather could see it protruding from her clenched fist. He would revel in his granddaughter's joy before giving her a warm hug and kisses that competed with her sticky ones.

"How sweet Yara's kisses were! They usually tasted like strawberries," Abdullah would mutter in anguish before his mind wandered off again.

In his first week with us, Abdullah nearly got me into terrible trouble. We were walking alongside a busy roundabout where expatriate workers were engaged in their usual task of pulling up the paving stones and replacing them with flowers. Ever since I had arrived in Oman, these workers had done nothing but replace the pavements with grass and flowers, or vice versa.

Abdullah suddenly stopped and froze in his tracks. Dropping his hand, I turned round to look at him. He was panting and his eyes were rigid in their sockets. His mouth began to tremble, followed by his hands and his entire body. It was the first time I had seen him like this; before, he had always been serene, as if nothing bad had ever befallen him. But at this moment, he seemed to have opened the pages of his life and begun rewriting its lines as if he were a completely different person. He ran toward the freshly planted flowers and began to pull them up, shouting at the astonished workers:

"Fools! You're planting flowers in the streets when it's bombs you should be planting so you'll die quickly. Your death will be painless, so quick you won't feel a thing or be afraid. It will leave behind a trail of smoke that reaches the sky, that everyone will see, just as God does. Anyway, He sees everything that happens. This smoke will plant you up there, perhaps inside a cloud. The cloud may rain and sow you in a land where the streets are planted not with flowers, but perhaps— perhaps—with bombs."

With great effort, I dragged Abdullah away from the traffic circle for fear the police would come after us and we'd find ourselves in an even greater predicament. Oh, my friend! Is being killed by a merciful bomb any different to dying from a poisoned dagger in the hand of a faithless lover? I dismiss the question and return to the bombs blossoming on the pavement. I witness many souls peacefully ascending skyward, scattered flesh, phone cameras, and renowned journalists, their faces filled with horror. I hear the screams of others fearing the same fate or mourning a loved one whose lips were destroyed by a bomb before he finished his sentence. I see faces rigid with shock, arms dangling beside bodies or thrown into the distance. Will the dead know the bomb was meant for them rather than for millions elsewhere?

One dies; another loses part of himself. Some are sad; others weep. Some become numb, and many feel and notice nothing. Those are the ones who don't deserve to die like heroes, their souls rising like smoke to choke the sky and our lungs. Instead, they should be left to expire like cowards beneath their warm blankets.

I feel deeply ashamed when I ask Abdullah to forget the past, to turn the page and make peace with life. I am overlooking the fact that forgetting is just a gigantic lie we tell ourselves and believe all too willingly. Though no one forces us to, we believe in that lie with all the innocence of first love, and the same foolishness. We believe in its beauty the way we believed in our first kiss and the wave of the traveller returning from a distant journey. I ask Abdullah to forget even as I am drowning in memory. With the same bitterness, he says in a choked voice:

"My friend, forgetting has no allure for a man like me. My eyes fill with tears whenever I imagine Yara running, her hair flowing down her back like a river suddenly rising to tease the wind, her little fingers trying to scoop up the falling stars, her laughter, her screams, her face that is here and yet gone. The loyal don't forget. How can fate be kind, comforting me while Yara's coffin is borne aloft and the angels compete to make her fly in paradise—a bird with wings of light and a body that tastes of strawberries? Tell the trees in paradise about me, my little one. Tell them I need shade; ask them to grow tall while you wait for me there. I promise to hide the candy so you can guess which hand, but I won't tell you it's in both my hands.

"I'm afraid, my daughter, but that fear did not start the day I lost you. I've been afraid ever since I learned that I was an Arab, afraid of something like the ghoul in my mother's bedtime stories, not like the happy endings she gave them each night. It reaches out like a long shadow, ending God knows where, plunging you into a morass of anxiety, tension, and retreat from the unknown. I've been chased by fear since my mother first told me there is a blood feud between me and everyone I love, and at any moment, I could be struck down by a bullet from an unexpected direction. I'm obsessed with the details of those directions, jumping out of my skin at the slightest sound. I've lived in fear since my mother warned me not to kill a friend to take his livelihood or his beloved. I've been afraid since I realized the word my mother called me—Arab—is a sin that will stay with me for my entire life, like a brand on my forehead or an extra finger on my right hand."

In this way, Abdullah abruptly stops talking to me and addresses himself to his daughter Yara or his father. I even hear him converse with his wife, asking her about Bakr, the son he never saw. Has Bakr grown up in paradise, or hasn't she delivered yet? Will she wait for Abdullah to take her to the hospital, or will she go into early labour like she did with Yara and have to call for Um Ismail, the midwife? It was Um Ismail who had delivered Abdullah, but he didn't know if she had died along with the others or was still delivering the babies of the local women who went into labour while their husbands were away working.

I feel queasy after every conversation with Abdullah. Contrary to what people think, I'm not on a hunger strike. I just have no appetite, or rather, everything turns my stomach. Sometimes the universe takes the shape of an absent loved one, and all of life disappears with them, or you search for your smile and find it stuck in a high window where you can't reach it.

I tell Abdullah about my little sister, who died when I was six. At the time, I didn't understand the meaning of death, and the atmosphere of grief was too great for anyone to pay attention to a six-year-old smiling naively at the mourners. I tell Abdullah how bashful I was when someone patted me on the head, how I smiled foolishly at the faces of the weeping women, how surprised I was at the cluster of mourners around my sister. I still remember the women hovering helplessly over her; their lamentation and wailing and all the other sounds that made me laugh; and finally, the acceptance of her death—when they washed and shrouded the body. All of it meant nothing to me. I cared only about the candy I had brought my sister from school, which was still in my palm. What would have happened if I had shouted at the top of my voice?

"Come here, little sister, I've brought you the candy you love!"

To this day, I am still a child of six. I have not learned to hide my laugh from the face of sadness or to dry my tears before they fall. I am as guileless now as then; my soul still warms at the thought of my father's gentle touch. But I no longer play football with the neighbourhood boys or dog my father's every footstep, and my brothers no longer sneak out of the house without me. I am an adult now, not the boy who dozed beside the mosque as he waited for his father to finish praying and take him home. I no longer chase the car that carries him off without a backward wave, and the neighbours don't need to drag me home when I run after him weeping. I don't quarrel with the local boys for excluding me from their games because my puny body can't withstand their deliberate roughhousing. Blood doesn't stream from my small nose when they kick it accidentally or on purpose. Even my nose has grown up with me, can you believe it? I have grown up, little sister, but pain has trapped my heart at the age of six.

These days, my mind wanders when I talk to Abdullah. Each of us is absorbed in his private sorrow. One will start speaking to the other but finish his conversation alone, addressing himself to the missing or the dead. Abdullah asks:

"Why do children die and leave us with candy on our hands and lips for the rest of our lives? If only the candy had died and left our loved ones behind! Yara might have cried a little when she couldn't have the sweets she loved, but then she would have forgotten and abandoned herself to the joy of childhood."

He chuckles as he recalls how naughty Yara used to climb the trees beside their house, standing on a branch and calling out to her mother:

"When will I grow wings and fly like a bird?"

"When you listen to your Mama and eat your food, then you'll grow up and get wings. Come down now, my sweet little bird."

Yara climbs down each time only after she has picked two pieces of fruit—one for herself and one for her brother Bakr. She won't eat her piece until her mother finishes the other, until she is certain both Bakr and his mother are enjoying her gift.

"When Bakr gets here, he'll sleep with me in my bed, and I'll give him strawberry candy."

"Babies don't eat sweets, Yara; they only drink milk."

"Why?"

"Because their mouths are little, and they don't have any teeth yet."

"I can share my teeth with my brother Bakr, look, Mama, I have lots of them."

At this point, Abdullah always stops talking and starts to sob.

"But in the end, it was death she shared with him—the flames and ashes, the piles of rubble and the loss. Even with my eyes shut, I can still see her charred body, her legs—torn from her body and thrown in different directions—and her hair, bleached gold by the sun just like mine. Can you believe I had blond hair when I was little? My hair refused to turn black; it only accepted its true nature once I had grown up. Yara and I aren't the only blonds in my country; most of the children are blond, too, maybe because the sun is so strong."

Abdullah calms down slightly, then resumes talking as we make our way back to the room we share with four others. It's not like the wooden room I lived in during my first job here; this one is concrete, with black iron bedsteads and a separate toilet.

"When America attacked Iraq after the disastrous Kuwait War, I begged God night and day to liberate Iraq. At the same time, my beloved father got so ill, we thought he was dying. I admit now that I thought he wouldn't survive, so I started bracing myself for his death. I divided my prayers into two groups—a group for my father and another for Iraq. One day, I decided to choose only one and pray for it with all my heart and soul, with all the faith and sincerity in me. Since I'd lost hope that God would spare my bedridden father, I chose Iraq. I couldn't hear my father's heartbeat over the beeping of the monitors, and I had faith in the Arabs, so I prayed for Iraq to be free once more.

"God was truly generous with us, and my father made a complete recovery. But Iraq did not. Like Palestine, it was lost, and now Syria, Libya, and Egypt are going the same way. Yemen too, my friend; its sons and brothers have lost it, and what's next, the Gulf? It also is withering away. The fall in oil prices is only the start of its collapse, and what then? America will claim victory, and so will Israel. And what will we Arabs get? Defeat, destruction, and death. We'll get what we don't want, and they'll get what they do.

"Forgive me, God, for not shouting at the top of my lungs every time I saw a Muslim weep, for not cursing the tyrants to their faces. Though it would have meant a bullet to my head, at least that would have spared me the suffering I'm feeling now.

"Don't hold me responsible, God, for the evil deeds of tyrants. I have never carried a weapon or turned one on a defenceless man. I have never fired a missile that obliterated the home of a happy family. I have never written a poem, a verse, or even a single word glorifying the murder of innocents by oppressors. It galls me that we take people like these as our role models and our religious authorities, when they have forced religion to bow down to the greed of rulers and the power of money.

"They say the West is more humane, and its churches opened their doors to refugees; many Muslims embraced Christianity after they lost faith in Islam, which had sustained them for so long. But when we killed those people in the name of religion, we also killed religion, though we carried on reciting poetry and boasting of our deeds that only diminished us.

"The West is no better than someone who plunges a perfumed knife into your heart. It conspired against us when we were strong, then welcomed us when we were weak, after its nations had kicked us back and forth like a football. But at least the West kills with one hand and strews flower-covered thorns with the other. The Arabs, by contrast, are still serving us up to death, one country after another. I think conspiracy theories are complete nonsense. No one can force you to do something against your will. It's idiotic for us to blame others and claim they plotted against us. We were easy targets, so they decided to gobble us up.

"We're no longer Muslims but sects: Ibadis, Sunnis, Shiites and so on. Our religion has splintered, and we've been divided into mini-states. We've killed each other and wronged each other, all while boasting: "Our dead are in paradise, while yours are in hell." What paradise and hell are we talking about?

"What arrogant fools we are! We are a rotten nation; we weep for Husain, though he was killed over a thousand years ago, but not for those being killed every day. While we're mourning Husain, we celebrate the anniversary of his death, as if we can no longer tell our weddings and funerals apart. We are like the proverb that says: 'He kills a man, then marches in his funeral'. We cry during our lavish banquets and mistake the sound of a slap for the hum of anthems. We go back a thousand years or more in time to punish ourselves for a crime committed by those who died long before our time, pardoning their misdeeds but never thinking of pardoning our own, which are beyond all forgiveness.

"We will go to any lengths to forget our present; we no longer care about it. People are dying; they are being killed, tortured, and displaced, while we keep on crying about what we lost a thousand years ago. What kind of half-witted nation are we, created from what foolish clay? Sadness has not taught us to confront injustice and take control of our destiny. We haven't learned from our past how to build our present before our future; we continue to weep like women for a lost glory we had no part in creating or destroying.

"Palestine taught us apathy and killed our chivalry and magnanimity. While Palestinian women are being murdered in front of the world, we watch it take place on the screen without blinking, and if we do blink, we replay the tape over and over so as not to miss a single scene. We watch out of curiosity, no more, reacting with indifference or perhaps unconcern, snivelling, railing, or cursing until we come across a dirty joke and laugh as if nothing has happened. They kill a child, and we watch it die. Later, we go in search of the meal we had postponed in order to watch the video. Damn that child! Had his time really come? Couldn't he have delayed his death until we had finished our tasteless meal?

"Death is all around us: on television, in the newspapers, online, on the roadways, too. Every day I realize what traitorous cowards we are, unfit to live on this earth. Our Creator is truly forgiving; if He were not, he would have caused the earth to swallow us up, commanded the sky to fall upon us in pieces, or struck us with a thunderbolt while we watched these videos without girding our loins and marching toward Palestine as one man with one heart. If those descendants of monkeys and pigs had known their actions would go unpunished, would they have done all these things? Of course not. But counting on our indifference, our fraternal hatreds, and our mundane ambitions, they wreaked havoc in Palestine."

Chapter Eight

The Construction Site

The dangerous act of leaving

God creates us all the same and blows His spirit into each of us, but we insist on lining up in the ranks to which mankind has assigned us.

The next morning, it seemed as if nothing had happened during the night. Even the foreman Sanjay, who normally held us accountable for every grain of sand, ignored the missing electrical wires and bags of cement. I was amazed, but who was I to worry about something that would bring me more hassle than praise if I mentioned it? How naive I am! Did I say praise? What praise would that be? My sleepless night is starting to affect me. I haven't heard a kind word since the day I arrived in this country, perhaps because I have shut myself in this room that grows more cramped and silent by the day.

I hand myself over to the foreman, whose voice seems more familiar to me than it did before. I had never paid much attention to him. He thought he was better than us and was forever patronizing us, even poor Ajay, whose hand he refused to shake though they came from the same country. When Ajay learned of my disapproval, he said with a smile:

"It's completely normal. He's higher caste than I am; he is from the Chopra, while I am a Dalit, an untouchable. India's Vedic society doesn't recognize us, though we were the country's original inhabitants. I have no idea how K.R. Narayanan, who was a Dalit, managed to be president of India from 1997 to 2002."

Ajay says this with a smile more of surprise than of pride. He talks about the caste system as something immutable, fixed for all time. Like his family name, his caste follows him wherever he goes.

"Did you know that if a Chopra violates a Brahmin's wife, they punish him by emasculating him and confiscating all his possessions? That's how they punished Sanjay's father after he assaulted his boss's wife. Sanjay was his father's last child; his wife left him after that. He finally drowned himself in the river to atone for his sin, but it will continue to follow his descendants, even after his death."

"But what if a Brahmin does the same thing to a non-Brahmin?"

"My friend, Brahmins can do whatever they like. Brahma created them from his mouth and ordered them to read the Vedas. No one can hold them to account, for they think they control everything."

Now I knew whose voice I'd heard the previous evening. I smirked. Was there anyone in this country who didn't steal? Everyone from the mighty to the lowly stole as much as his pocket would hold, each pocket expanding according to the importance of its owner. And however trustworthy and loyal these people claimed to be, their claims were only lip service. Who could believe the foreman would dare to steal from Mr. Kapoor? He followed Kapoor around like his shadow, parroting his every word.

My smile shrank when it met the foreman's stinking breath. It seemed he had been too busy celebrating last night's crime to clean his disgusting mouth. I dashed off to haul the bags of cement. My mind was blank, or perhaps it was so stuffed with things that they cancelled each other out for lack of space. The previous night passed unmentioned, with no reckoning or coronation for its protagonists, as if nothing had happened, to the point that I almost forgot it.

I used to go to sleep each night before the others so as to avoid getting drawn into anything untoward. It had never occurred to me that men denied the chance to exercise their most basic male roles— or more precisely, their sexual functions—would resort to anything to relieve their bodily needs. Though I could understand those who relieved their desires in their hands, there was no way I could excuse Babu, who used to leer at the women who came to admire the results of our handiwork. He claimed that some of them were hunting the scent of a man—and how many scents they could find in a building where sweat blended with lust, fatigue, and loneliness! I nearly slapped him when he whispered:

"See that girl who's acting so flirty? She's an easy target. Just one word and she'd give any of us the keys to her heart and her body."

He pointed out that, judging from her body, she was clearly getting on, but she was still strikingly beautiful, and according to Babu— that self-declared expert on women—her flirtatiousness meant she would spread her legs for anyone. Despite her age, he added, she was still unmarried. Her father had refused to marry her off, since he had found no one willing to pay the asking price for her beauty, which had once been surpassing and was still clearly visible. When I expressed surprise at Babu's detailed knowledge, he told me that the expatriate workers talked about nothing but the private lives of the residents in the villages where they worked. "Just imagine what they know: what people eat, what they hoard, how many rooms their houses have and how many people each room holds, who has a double bed and who sleeps apart like strangers."

Disgusted, I turned and walked away, at a loss for words to describe this man's sleaziness. Was it true? Did the workmen really gossip with the maids about household secrets? According to Babu, they even knew which wives were "starved for love"; which sons behaved decently and which gave their families a hard time; whose daughters were respectable and whose followed their appetites. Even the day labourers stuck their noses into everything they saw, passing judgment on relationships and sizing up people and property. One of them might even venture to ogle a housewife after leaving her home.

Though I was exhausted, my constant anxiety and troubled sleep meant I awoke at the slightest movement from a workmate, even if he was only turning over or adjusting his position. In any case, I doubted there was much rest for foreigners who spent their days between sand, cement, and the foreman's verbal abuse or noxious breath. One night, I awoke to feel Babu stepping over me. It didn't seem that he was headed for the toilet, since that wouldn't require so much stealth, and it was unlike him to be considerate of others. Ever since I had first met him, he had irritated everyone so much that he did not have a single friend.

I let him go out undisturbed, unaware he had roused me from my torpor, and followed him. Perhaps he had played a role in what happened the previous night, especially since he was now entering the building we had almost finished, which was only waiting for us to install the electrical appliances. But the quiet and darkness didn't suggest Babu was going to repeat last night's events.

I gave him a head start before I went into the building, where I was surprised to find the same girl that Babu had described as "hunting the scent of a man, any man." I felt dizzy, and my blood almost exploded from my nose. The ground trembled, and my feet seemed to have turned to lead, so I started to drag them, my shoes scraping the ground.

Despite the racket I was making, Babu paid me no more heed than he would a phantom cloud passing through the dark of a moonless night. But the girl's face betrayed confusion, as if this were her first time colluding with a man to violate her innocent world. With a repulsive laugh, Babu said:

"No worries. If you want her, you can have her when I'm done."

I spat in his face. I wanted to shout at him: "I have never eaten anyone's leftovers," but afraid of hurting the girl's feelings, I bit my tongue, which merely twitched silently inside my mouth. Grabbing the girl's hand, I dragged her out of the building. Not daring to look at her directly, I told her to take me to her house so I could make sure she arrived before her absence was noticed, and we could bury this night along with everything else we had lost.

While Babu stayed in the deserted building, I left with the girl, never imagining how Babu would revenge himself on me. The long road to the girl's house gave way to a calm broken only by her hoarse, stifled sobs. For my part, I couldn't bring myself to say a word for fear of unleashing the pain I felt. My heart was like a balloon ready to burst from the weight of injustice and oppression.

"He promised to take me to his country and marry me. He swore he had saved up enough money for us to live a good life. Over there, they don't care about all these outdated customs that have deprived me of my most basic rights—a small family, a loving husband, and children for my old age. I never thought about where things might lead. Nobody cares about me, so why should I care about them? What have I got to lose? Nothing. On the contrary, I'll gain a husband who can give me the life I want.

"I'm not dreaming of a perfect life or a life of luxury. I know I'll have a hard time with the differences in culture and the standard of living, and it won't be easy to communicate with his family because we don't speak the same language. I'll lose my family here and never be able to come back. But I don't feel like I belong in this family anyway. They pay no attention to me; they only care about their own interests and what they can get out of me. I'll accept whatever happens with love, because that's what a righteous wife should do.

"I'm tired of being the family drudge. My father wants to get back what he invested in my upbringing. My brothers want me to wait on their wives. My mother can't control the household, so she pushes me around instead: 'Don't go out! Don't wear that! Don't speak! Don't meet anyone!' Everything is off-limits, everything is forbidden, and every order has to be carried out without discussion or argument.

"Even my neighbour Heba got married, in spite of the scandal she caused when she was twenty-seven and had a baby without being married. I can still remember how she suffered—precious, untouchable Heba, paragon of honour and virtue, who came from an irreproachable family. They had refused to marry her off because no one was good enough for them. They never expected the blow to come from inside their own household, from the servant they had trusted as if he were not a man. They treated him like a slave who wouldn't dare look his master in the face. As a result, he stole Heba's heart, and she gave him her body.

"Her family didn't see how her eyes shone when they summoned him to bring coffee or serve a guest who'd just arrived. Her mother didn't notice when Heba sneaked out of bed to spend the night with him. And even Heba didn't notice how her belly was curving or try to hide it, since she had never imagined this could happen. She loved him, but neither she nor her family believed a slave could impregnate his master until the day the doctor asked her, 'Are you married?' and her mother answered, 'No, we haven't yet found anyone suitable for a girl of her lineage'.

"The doctor was silent. She ran some tests on Heba and made a call. Heba and her mother waited for the results. The police arrived and told them to come down to the station. There, the shock hit:

she could either marry the help or spend several months in jail. Even though she loved him and their baby, she chose prison. Maybe it was her family's choice; I'm not sure. In the final months of her pregnancy, she was released, but only after pledging not to harm her child, to save her family from being thrown in prison, too. Her family put up with her until the child was well on his way to seeing the light of day. Her pain worsened, but there was to be no hospital for her. Everything had been decided; besides a small lamp, only her mother and an elderly maid were present. Whenever she complained, her mother would spit insult after insult at her. The stabs grew sharper; the baby insisted on coming. How could the maid smile with such insolence when Heba was being torn apart?

"'There's his head! He's coming. Your first grandchild, Madam!'"

"'Shut up, you stupid woman! Don't you dare say that ever again!'"

His head peeked out at the world, his grandmother's curses drowning out his scream of fright.

"'You slut! He's black—black!'

"As Heba's body shook with pain, the child struggled with every ounce of his being to live. His tiny feet still touched her body, kicking as they fought death, but the white hand pressing down on his neck was stronger. His feet fell quiet with the umbilical cord still hidden inside her, almost before he had drawn breath. Her mother's single blow to her belly was enough to knock Heba unconscious. Were the words she had overheard real, or had she dreamt them?

"'The bastard is dead; he was stillborn. 'La hawla wa la quwwata illa billah,'" the mother muttered in forced condolence. "'Bury him on the farm, under the small palm tree; it needs fertilizer. Graveyards are too pure for such bastards.'

"And even though Heba's story was the talk of the town, she did get married, not to a Shaykh or the son of one as her father hoped, nor to the strapping youth she'd imagined, but to a randy old man who saw her as his last chance to renew his youth and lord it over her. She got married, and now she has seven children. She no longer looks for her son's grave among the young palm trees on their big farm; the trees are all grown now. Just imagine: Heba has seven children, and I don't even have one. She calls all the shots at home, and her husband is wrapped around her little finger. Though he couldn't control her, he was able to occupy her body and enjoy it whenever he liked—her 'sinful' body, as the neighbours call it, because it's been touched by another man—while I've stayed like a palm tree grown prematurely old, unwatered and my fruit unharvested.

"I want to get married. I'm forty now, and my youth is nearly over. I worry constantly that I'll grow old alone and spend the rest of my life waiting on my sisters and their husbands, raising their children, but never smelling the scent of my own child. I came here to meet Babu so we could agree on our escape plan, but he asked me to give myself to him first. That's why we argued: I don't want to be like Heba, dogged by shame, hiding my face in the dirt—that is, if my family doesn't bury me in it first. I want a family to care for, a husband I love, and children I chase after to make them get dressed or eat supper. If Babu and I hadn't quarrelled, you wouldn't have found me here. We would already be in his country, celebrating the life we were dreaming of."

She prattled on and on. Some of what she was saying I could take in, and some of it didn't make sense, but I had nothing to say. Did she really think that vile creature Babu wanted to marry her? How had he found his way into her heart, or was her heart irrelevant, given her desperation? How could she say nothing about his offer to give her to me after he had finished with her? Why do fathers close every door in their daughters' faces, leaving them nowhere to turn but to scum like Babu?

"This is where I live," she said, not looking at me. At that moment, I could only gather my courage, grasp her hand and whisper in a voice I hoped she could hear: "Please, don't come back. He's a liar and a cheat. Promise me you won't come back."

She dropped my hand and slipped into her house. I waited a moment before admitting there was nothing I could do, then headed home. She had gone, but the coolness of her hand gradually stole through my veins until I realized I was shaking. This was the worst night I had spent since arriving in this country. How different it is to steal money than to steal a body; to take something only your accomplice will discover, versus leaving a mark on your victim that time will not erase. Even if nobody else notices, it is like robbing someone of his life and dreams on his deathbed.

It is always girls who pay the price for their fathers' greed. Fathers close every door to their daughters' desires, because they are determined to sell them to the highest bidder and extract as much life from their bodies as they spent on their upbringing. As the years pass, the price keeps going up, until one day the daughters realise their worth has started to decline. Nobody wants them anymore, and all the men who longed to sip their sweet nectar walk away like merchants deserting an auction for spoiled merchandise. Look at that tall, lissom beauty, her milky complexion tinged with rose—an onlooker can almost picture the river of blood flowing beneath her translucent skin. The years have marched on by, leaving her body to wither, untouched by any hands but her own.

I entered the room I shared with the others. They were all awake rather than sprawled on the floor as usual. I couldn't decipher their stares, which were fixed on me in search of something to confirm what Babu had just told them. Returning before me, he had claimed to have seen me with a girl in the building. That was his revenge for my preventing his crime. No one spoke a word to me, but Babu's gloating smile made it plain.

Though I said nothing, I was so angry that I could no longer stand to be there. I collected some of my belongings to help identify me in case they found no distinctive marks on my body, such as my birthmark. My mother used to claim it had been caused during her pregnancy, when my father hadn't brought her the fresh dates she craved. Because of that, a prominent dark mark appeared below my right shoulder. It had gradually begun to disappear, though, God denying me even this great blessing. It seemed I would have to leave this world stripped of everything, even a dark birthmark that could identify my lifeless body.

I fled without deciding on a destination that might receive me. Anywhere, no matter how bad, would be better than suffocating in this foul place. Walking was not enough; the anger inside me was unbearable. I wanted to scream, to surrender my voice to the wind, though who would hear a tear-laden voice borne on the breeze? I gave my legs free rein and began to run.

Chapter Nine

The Date Farm

Mukhtar's flight

Everything has a diploma, even death. Only life won't certify that you have completed it.

Three months had passed since I started working on the farm. I had mastered the different methods for cultivating date palms and harvesting their fruit, as well as for handling and pruning every type of tree. Am Sulayman was unfailingly generous. Not only did he pay our wages, but we shared his breakfast, and his wife brought us lunch every day. The only meal we were responsible for was supper. I even started to gain back some of the weight I had lost, although we worked from dawn prayer until a little before sunset, except on the days I joined Am Sulayman's visits to check on his friends. Although I always completed my work before departing so as to leave none for Taj al-Islam, he invariably got angry and grumbled that he had to do everything himself.

Am Sulayman began to enjoy my company, and I started to accompany him on his daily rounds, which lasted from afternoon prayers until nearly sunset. Like all his contemporaries in this sleepy neighbourhood tucked away among the date plantations, he would gather with his lifelong friends outside one of their homes to watch the passers-by and local children, whose antics lifted the men's spirits with almost palpable joy. Whenever a group of kids sped by on their bicycles at death-defying speed, the old men would laugh and shout:

"What's the rush? Look at us—that's what we did, and our lives were gone before we knew it."

The conversation would have taken a darker turn if Am Khalfan, the biggest joker in the group, had not interjected:

"Who're you calling old? Ya Shaykh, I'm still thirty! Don't be fooled by my white hair. Part of it came from fear and the rest from all my bright ideas."

They would all laugh contentedly despite the bygone years that waved at them across the horizon whenever they met. They were invigorated by these regular meetups, where they traded stories and jokes and reminisced about their youthful pranks and dalliances. They also played a board game in which I joined. When I won, I could see the teenager in Am Sulayman's heart jumping for joy. I deliberately started winning just for the thrill of seeing him return to his youth, when his hair was a glossy black and his spine was still straight.

As we played, the men and I moved a pebble from one square to another, or rather, from one hole to another, in a game of hawalees. Hawalees, a traditional game favoured by the older generation in all the poor neighbourhoods, was like chess. Everyone gathered around two players, following their moves and applauding as they awaited their turn. There were no pawns or king; the pieces all had the same value, and a player won by removing all the other player's pebbles from the board. I used to conclude my victories by saying "Checkmate!", after which Am Sulayman would turn and rebuke me:

"There's no checkmate in this game, Mukhtar."

Hawalees was the most beautiful thing left in the lives of these men, who were as vibrant as flowers that refused to wilt, still fragrant despite their advancing years. The best part of these gatherings was how they lifted my spirits. Whether the men were exchanging anecdotes, memories, or snippets of news, they threw themselves into everything, from politics and hawalees—which no one ever lost because they competed with such affection—to the jokes they found irresistible and stories that were always about each other, never their children, families, or other men. They were a close-knit group, and because they were always so lively and contented, I never expected to find Death in their midst. The first time I saw his spectre looming in the distance, the friends—to my astonishment—winked at one another.

"Here comes the Dead One!"

At first, I thought that was his real name, but I kept quiet. There was no way a father would name the son for whom he had longed the "Dead One," as if he had foreseen the boy's death or wished it upon him. Perhaps they were comparing him to a dead person because of his waxy pallor; yes, that was it, his face must be as pale as a corpse's. But when the Dead One approached, I saw that he was younger and livelier than the rest of them. Curiosity knocked inside my head. Peering out from my eyes and waving to get my attention, it whispered: "Ask them why they say he's dead. If you don't, I'll stand here until they see me."

Why have I become so nosy since I started spending the evenings with Am Sulayman and his friends?

"Fine, I'll ask them, but go inside before anyone sees you, if they haven't already, while they introduce me to their dead friend," I said to the nagging voice, but the Dead One spotted Curiosity and pointed at me, laughing:

"Just look at him! He's dying to know why you called me the Dead One when you saw me coming. I know you start making fun of me the moment you see me. So how do you like my new name?"

Though he was joking, I was bewildered. It felt like he could read my mind. Was he truly dead, and his soul was standing in for him? They all joined in his laughter, even Am Sulayman, who didn't usually laugh at me. The Dead One grasped my chin and turned my face toward him to get my attention, which was already riveted.

"I'm dead, Mukhtar; believe me, I'm dead."

As I gaped at him, the group chorused:

"It's true! He really is dead."

The Dead One quickly resumed his story before my heart stopped or I mistook him for a wandering soul that Heaven had not yet welcomed in.

"Pull yourself together. What are you frightened of? I'm not bewitched—magic died out a long time ago. I really am dead, but only according to the official records.

"Three years ago, my brother travelled abroad. He was only eight months older than me, and therein lies the tale. Since my parents were in a rush to bring me into the world, my mother got pregnant with me right after her forty days of post-partum confinement, and claimed for the rest of her life that I'd been an accident."

He winked slyly at me as a smile stole onto his lips. They were covered by a thick moustache that reached down to join his long beard, of which he was clearly very proud.

"Do you believe pregnancies happen by accident? Don't worry; a mother's word is gospel, and we have to believe it. What matters is that, like my brothers, I was in a hurry to arrive, and my mother gave birth to me in her sixth month, only a month after she learned she was expecting. She thought her periods had stopped because she was nursing; she didn't realize a naughty little one was hiding inside her belly. I wasn't expected to live; in those days, it was rare for babies born at seven or eight months to survive, let alone one born at six. But somehow I broke the mould and survived. Whenever death came for me, I would snarl at him and tell him to get lost. That was how death gave in to this naughty child and allowed him to live a good life. Ho ho! The days of childhood are long gone, but I'm still naughty. What do you say, friends?"

Am Khalfan elbowed him.

"Finish your story. This poor fellow's face is white with fear. It seems he hasn't heard about us Omanis and our names. I'll tell him once you're done."

"The important thing is that my brother—God rest his soul—decided to make the Umrah pilgrimage. His passport had expired, but since I looked exactly like him, he didn't bother to renew it, or maybe he was too lazy, since there was an alternative to hand. He travelled to Mecca on my passport, but on the way back, his group was involved in a car crash and my brother was killed. May he rest in peace! They issued his death certificate in my name, of course, since he was carrying my passport. He was buried there so he could remain near the Blessed Prophet, as is customary for anyone who dies in Mecca or Medina. Dying in the Holy Places is an honour God grants only to the deserving, so it would be a disservice to send that person home for burial. Sometimes I wonder if even the Prophet thinks the man buried beside him is my brother, not me."

"Be quiet, Mr. Dead. Don't blaspheme!" Am Khalfan interrupted, but the Dead One ignored him:

"For the last three years, I've been requesting a certificate to prove I'm alive, but they tell me that no such thing exists. There is a certificate for everything but life. Even death gets its share of certificates, but life remains something secondary, not worth a second glance. If only people knew that this life has no meaning."

He looked at Am Marhun and chuckled.

"Marhun, do you think Mukhtar will believe the story of your name?"

I turned toward him, my face filled with questions. He continued, laughing so hard that I wouldn't have understood a word if Am Sulayman hadn't explained it to me later, on our way home.

Am Marhun's story was an extraordinary one. All his brothers born before him had died before the age of two. One lived for a month, another for six. The third boy was luckier; he lasted a year and nine months before death carried him off. The fourth never saw the light of day because his mother miscarried in her fourth month. When Marhun was born, those of wise counsel and religion urged the family to pledge him to a jinn so he would live, and that is exactly what they did. They named the child Marhun, "the pledged one," after promising him to a kind-hearted female jinn who resided in one of the ghaaf trees. The ghaaf is a semi-desert tree that needs very little water because its roots reach deep into the soil to quench its thirst. Known for its longevity, the ghaaf can live more than two hundred years and reach a height of over twenty metres.

Every night, his family put Marhun inside a basket of palm fronds and suspended it from the branches of the ghaaf tree until daybreak. Before the birds awoke, Marhun was brought back inside, after screaming and crying his heart out with no tender hand to console him. The villagers believed that the jinn was nursing him so he wouldn't feel hunger.

This went on for an entire week, after which Marhun was returned to his mother and promptly fell asleep. After that, strangely, he no longer cried at night. People said that the jinn took him each night to nurse him, leaving a baby-shaped log in the crib that no one dared touch lest the jinn grow angry and refuse to return him. Why didn't they realize that the child had grown used to being alone at night? Even at that tender age, he understood no one would come when he cried, so he learned to be quiet. Didn't they worry that a viper would bite him or a bird snatch him as he hung on the tree branch like a new-born chick with no parents to care for it or even feed it?

Amazingly, Marhun survived, as did his neighbour Mabyu', the "Sold One," whose family hadn't just pledged him, but sold him outright to a different family after his three older brothers died in infancy. Mabyu' was sold so he could live, as if to trick the King of Death into thinking: "Hold on! This isn't the son of So-and-so, whose children's souls I usually take." And although it was entirely a matter of psychology, the family—as the Prophet has promised—were rewarded for their good intentions.

Am Sulayman himself told me his story, which was similar to those of his friends. He had been married twice, and both his wives had died giving birth to their first child. Am Sulayman wanted to remarry, but the idea filled him with terror, since it meant his wife and future child would die, or so his heart told him. There was an ancient tree to which the local people made offerings in the belief that the Muslim jinn who inhabited it could help them obtain their hearts' desires. People advised Am Sulayman to marry this tree and spend the night with it to try and overcome his complex about his wives' deaths. Am Sulayman actually signed a nuptial contract with the tree and spent a whole night with it. He then took a new wife, who gave birth and did not die. Poor Am Sulayman! How had he felt toward his tree-bride, and how had they spent their wedding night?

"But Am Sulayman, do you honestly believe that marrying the tree had anything to do with the matter?" I asked one day. He looked at the ground and shook his head ruefully.

"Those days were the Jahiliyya, the Dark Ages, my son. We were ignorant, and it was easy to fill our heads with superstitions. In a moment of weakness, a person was capable of doing anything. Thank God for the blessings of Islam and science. If it hadn't been for them, we would not have shed those superstitions, but handed them down to our children just as they were handed down to us."

My mind wandered for a bit. Would I have resorted to magic or the jinn if someone had suggested it could help me win Houria, or would I have mocked the idea? Who could believe someone had married a tree to ensure the survival of his future wife?

Am Sulayman was extremely perceptive. He came to know when I was out of sorts and distracted, and any thoughts of Houria were certain to put me in a foul mood. He blamed my unhappiness on the fact that I was a foreigner far from home and family, and he regularly tried to console me.

"There is no shame in working, my son, and emigrating is a way to earn a living. Just be patient until you reach your goal. I too emigrated for work even before I reached puberty. Because minors weren't allowed to work abroad, we would claim to be the sons of some distant relative or a neighbour employed in a nearby country, joining him there after he got us passports in his name. The same thing is happening now with some Omanis, the ones who came here from other countries. They give their names to their relatives back home and claim they are Omani, so they can bring them here for a better life.

"I'd only just begun shaving when I started working abroad, an emigre with no family or identity. My story may be hard to believe, but it's true. When I was a boy, I worked overseas in petrol stations serving tea and coffee to the guests of my boss until my lungs were soaked with petrol fumes. Over there, they looked down on us, just as we despise immigrants here. We had to move from job to job just to earn enough for our families to put up with our long absence. Growing up, we had no chance for any fun. We couldn't even communicate with our loved ones except through letters that someone would carry home for us, our money and love tucked into an envelope sealed with our sweat and homesickness. Our wives and mothers couldn't read, so we had to share our secrets with strangers. When we sent a letter home, the longing in it would scorch the person who read it and turn cold before it reached the ears of our loved ones.

"When oil started to transform our country's economy, we came back home to work, but what kind of work was it? All we knew was what we had learned in the village schools. We didn't bring any reference letters with us, since what kind of references can waiters or petrol-station attendants get? We were forced to work for foreign experts in our own country, since no one believed a local could actually be productive, and he wasn't given a chance even if he had a university degree. This 'foreigner complex' persists even today. The foreigners are the experts and the directors, and every Omani has to be an understudy to them until the day he retires. There is no way an Omani can replace a foreign expert, even if the foreigner gets his expertise from the marginalized Omani.

"When the government decided to designate certain jobs for Omanis, they were only menial positions, like driving petrol tankers or water lorries. Even those weren't safe from the foreigners; they owned the cars and hired Omanis to drive them. As for senior and managerial positions, they were still reserved for the foreign *ex-perts.*" He drew out the word to underscore his bitterness.

"Can you believe it? My elder son Abdullah has a doctorate in geology, but he reports to a foreign boss. The irony is that my son does all the work, while the so-called expert gets all the thanks and praise. My son often comes to me in despair, saying he wants to resign. I don't like his defeatism, so I have to be tough on him. He has to stay, like a bone blocking their airways, until they choke on our determination and our right to be here. This is our country, Mukhtar, and it's the foreigners who should leave.

"Excuse me, Mukhtar, I don't mean people like you, I mean those who are sucking the blood and marrow out of our country. If the oil wells ran dry, they'd just pick themselves up and go home to enjoy a comfortable retirement. They're the ones who've taken over trade, who monopolize our natural resources. They've become our masters and we the foreigners here. None of us can get his rights unless a foreigner approves and deigns to toss him the scraps."

It's all right, my dear Am Sulayman, I said to myself, merely giving him a smile I tried to make sincere. I knew he was fond of me, so I didn't want him to see how his comments had offended me, though his points were well-taken. I sought refuge in a white cloud that lingered overhead, floating by itself in the endless sky. It's all right; like that lonesome cloud in its vast sky, I am indeed a foreigner here. But I am not one of those opportunists. I came here only to escape the suffering that had slipped into my heart and taken my dreams by surprise, dreams I had built year after year until they merged into one—unlike the Arabs, who never could agree on a common dream. And because dreams don't live long, mine were suddenly assassinated by the very woman in whose hands I had prepared myself to blossom.

Taj al-Islam had trained me to go out in the evening after prayer and open up the irrigation channels between the trees, returning about ten o'clock to turn off the water. Then we would cook and eat our supper together, sharing our laughter and woes. Taj al-Islam's habits became mine, and although I hadn't found a single Arab to talk to, Taj al-Islam and his companions would speak in their broken Arabic out of consideration for me. In turn, I picked up a few words of their language, which occasionally slipped into their conversations.

"This is the first time I've seen an Arab working on a farm. This kind of manual labour doesn't suit Arabs with their tender skins," one of the men from the evening gatherings said with an enquiring look. All I could do was hold out my skin for his inspection, as I muttered:

"Some Arabs have skin as tough as cactus, my friend—you'd better look out for the thorns."

I laughed, and they all joined in my laughter, mirthless for reasons they did not care to know. After all, it's good to laugh for no reason sometimes, to relieve our souls of a hot day's labour.

I went back to riding a bicycle as I had in my rowdy youth, accompanying Taj al-Islam on his evening rounds. I learned to use my free evenings to repair appliances or install electricity and water in houses, drawing on my previous experience. Taj al-Islam directed me toward this extra work so I could exploit every moment of my time in exile for my future benefit. I became adept at pretending I could do anything, even if I knew less than the person asking me. Everything becomes easy with effort and experience. If you didn't know how to fix something, you just claimed it needed a new part. And if you replaced the things you couldn't repair, people thought you had fixed them. These weren't particularly clever tricks, but they fooled people who trusted you blindly.

Couldn't things have carried on like this, with these small shared pleasures? I doubt it. Life, which had the habit of burning me whenever I smiled, was bound to leave its mark on every experience I had. One morning, I climbed a khisab palm to pick its dates, which ripen after all the other trees have laid down their burden of many months. As I was bending the boughs downwards to make it easier to pick the still-tender fruit, Taj al-Islam rushed up to me, shouting in alarm:

"Inspectors! The inspectors are coming! Get out of here!"

Chapter Ten

The Furniture Workshop

A surprise loss

Everything loses its value when you are alone.

I'm so tired. I feel like the last creature alive, carrying the weight of the world on my shoulders, taking my sweat and my shovel, my fear and my anxiety with me wherever I go. I dare not look behind me when sounds seem to be drawing near. I know I'm the only person left on earth, and any sound would only be the hallucinations of an exile spending his final moments alone, or a delusion brought on by my conviction that I am about to die.

Following my father's advice, I always carry an olive sprig to plant in case Judgment Day should catch me unawares, with no good deeds to intercede for me in the Hereafter. For a moment, I am master of all I survey—I am the judge and the condemned, the king and his subjects—but it is all worthless. Everything loses its value when you are alone. No heart beats along with yours; no voice recites its prayers for you; you know you will neither be missed nor mourned.

I wonder if my father realized, when he named me Muhammad Mukhtar, that he had decreed for me a fate as complex as my name. My father stamped his love for our great and merciful Prophet—whom he confidently asserted was sent in mercy to humankind—upon the names of all his sons, hoping we would resemble the Prophet and emulate him. If someone criticized my father for giving us all the same name, he would simply reply that even if God had granted him ten sons, he would have named every one of them Muhammad. He added a second name to differentiate us, so my brothers were called Muhammad Amin, Muhammad Mustafa, and Muhammad Sadiq, and I was known as Muhammad Mukhtar.

Mukhtar, as everyone referred to me, was an homage to Umar Mukhtar, the celebrated Libyan resistance fighter who refused to surrender to the Italian occupation but continued fighting it until his final years, when the Italians finally captured and executed him. Later, when I looked into the life of the man whose name I was honoured to bear, I learned that the Italians had offered to pardon him and spare his life if he asked his followers to surrender and abandon their struggle. Umar Mukhtar refused, choosing a martyr's death rather than a life of ignominy, holding his head high as in his famous maxim:

"Be noble and never bow your head, no matter how compelling the circumstances, for you may not have a chance to raise it again."

Revered both in life and in death, Umar Mukhtar gained the immortality he had sought. After a photograph of him—a man of more than seventy—hanging from the gallows circulated, the resistance picked up its pace, lasting until the Libyans managed to expel the Italians from their country. By extraordinary coincidence, Umar Mukhtar and I had both been born on the twentieth of August, the month when great men and heroes enter the world, as my father used to say.

God rest your soul, Abi, you always wanted me to have an illustrious future. You hoped I would be like the Prophet Muhammad or Umar Mukhtar; you hoped history would immortalize me and people remember me as they do the heroes whose lives and exploits you were forever relating. You did not know what a disappointment I would be, a coward who was unable to ward off sorrow and despair. Though I ran from my weakness, fear pursued me wherever I went.

My father always slipped our names into his prayers one by one, asking God to grant each boy the good things he wished for him and to protect him from what he feared. But my father died, and his prayers died with him. They no longer surround us like a protective shield, warding off harm.

The rest of the workers and I gathered to discuss what was to become of us after our colleague Mujahid had absconded with the funds for the project. Silence dominated the meeting: imposing its presence, dictating its terms and conditions, and laying out all the scenarios. None of us dared to break its thrall, engage it in discussion, or amend its agenda; we were all sunk in cowardice. Fear engenders cowardice, and life in exile breeds only fear. Who were we to think and talk and decide? We knew Mujahid had put the owner of the shop in dire straits and the owner would end up in court, since he had given Mujahid total control of everything—"needle and thread," as the saying goes—in exchange for a paltry sum at the end of each month. This was the common practice among Omanis who wanted to enter commerce without incurring risk or loss. They failed to understand that the real losses would come through embezzlement and settled instead for the scraps of profit tossed to them. Those scraps were all Shaykh Mansur had gained in exchange for lending his name to Mujahid's work, the quality of which was so good that everyone, from the owner down to Mujahid's colleagues and fellow workers like us, had trusted him blindly.

Although Mujahid had come here fleeing the fires of war, he brought its embers with him and wanted to extinguish them in the hearts of everyone around him. I once believed that a person who had suffered could not inflict pain on others, but Mujahid proved how wrong I was. He had lost his home and profession; he had gone from being a doctor to upholstering used furniture. Like me, a man with a degree in architecture, Mujahid also had a university degree, but a more prestigious one. Whenever any of us ventured to mention our qualifications to our employers, they would say: "If you're not happy, you can leave." So you swallowed your degree in strangled silence and carried on working, because you knew that many others coveted your job and your wages, and you could be replaced within days or even hours by someone willing to work for less. Unlike you, however, they would not suffer from this crushing sense of inferiority that will grind like a millstone until it destroys every bead of dignity on your forehead and reduces your humanity to the dirt you came from.

Mujahid hadn't just taken money; he had taken our dreams, the future we'd imagined during the long, dark nights of insomnia and conversations trapped on our lips, which were blue from cold. He had taken the sweethearts who waited for us back home as they pictured their children, toys in their hands, growing up in their own small houses rather than jammed into the flats of their relatives. He had taken the medications our mothers patiently awaited, the houses for which we had not yet laid a single stone, our souls and the laughter we had so long imagined.

The kind-hearted boss—I am not sure if he was kind or merely naive, since he should never have trusted someone so completely—switched off his phone to evade the clients that Mujahid had fleeced while promising to fulfil their requests with the professionalism they had come to expect from him. In fact, Mujahid had just given the orders. We were the ones who laboured night and day under the heavy wood, following his instructions and the photographs of opulent furniture with which he hoodwinked people into buying his goods. As if by magic, our hands— or Mujahid's, people thought—transformed each ramshackle piece of furniture into a rare masterpiece specially tailored for each client. Now we either had to complete those orders for free or abandon our generous boss to prison to pay the price for his kindness and his trust in someone who did not deserve it. It was a difficult choice, which had to be made quickly, but we were neither suited nor prepared to do so.

Silence wandered among us, searching for the exit, carrying documents we had neither signed nor stamped. No one dared mutter or speak sharply to its stony face. Its eyes continued drilling into each of us in turn, while we sat as if we had been crucified and the birds were pecking out our brains. All that remained of us was our eyes, staring into the distance at dreams that had evaporated in an instant. We were so rooted to the spot that none of us would have dared change places even if his chair squeaked when he fidgeted. Nor would we have looked at him in irritation, since any of us could have made the same sound if we had so much as thought of moving.

Each of us drifted on his private sea, avoiding his confused companions lest they block the flow of his dreams, though he knew they were not the dreams he'd had before "that damned Mujahid", as Marwan called him, had absconded. We silently echoed the phrase like a litany of despair: "Damned Mujahid, damned Mujahid, damned Mujahid".

Finally, silence managed to escape through the opening Marwan gave it when his left leg was seized by cramp. Crying out, Marwan stretched his leg and pressed it with a hand in a desperate attempt to relieve the pain. At first, I looked at him askance, suspecting he had invented the cramp to release silence from the circle to which we had confined it. But the pain in Marwan's eyes was so clear that I dashed over to help him, while the others merely stood around and watched us until the cramp subsided, leaving his leg in peace. The leg had suffered quite enough humiliation, and any more pain could have resulted in a resounding crash you knew everyone would ignore, though they might commiserate briefly before heading off in search of their own dreams.

The irony was that Mujahid had gained everyone's confidence, all of us regarding him as a true "mujahid," or freedom fighter. Emerging from the bowels of war, he had arrived here cloaked in its revolution like a story-book hero. The only employee entrusted with money and secrets, he had now made off with it all, taking our savings and our bandages, leaving us with gaping wounds and tongues stripped of their secret tales and the words we had spent a lifetime acquiring. He could have taken just the money; why did he have to take everything? Now we would have to work and learn again, gather money and reformulate our sentences, and try to remember the stories we had told him before forgetting them, certain they were safely beyond reach in a deep well.

I wonder, is he now mocking our despondent voices with a rich girl whose body he purchased with our sweat, filling her ear with our stories and exploring her flabby contours with our money? No, he will choose a firm, young body. With our money, he can have his pick; with our dreams, he will brighten his life with the rainbow colours we sought behind every weeping, scudding cloud.

As we stood there in confusion, Shaykh Mansur came in. Neither silence nor Marwan's leg cramp had distracted us from the fear buffeting us, a fear to which we gave in with a servility I had always abhorred in myself. Yet now here I was, sharing it with my companions at this very moment. We responded to Shaykh Mansur's greeting, our voices barely audible. Out of respect, we pulled ourselves to our feet, though the seconds it took to stand up felt like an hour. None of us dared look at him for fear he would see the mixture of confusion, uncertainty, and defeat in our eyes.

Shaykh Mansur remained silent for so long that I stole a glance at him, only to find his eyes boring into my chest.

Chapter Eleven

The Café

A falling-out

You are free to decide, so take the decision that will keep your head held high.

Mukhtar

Hajj Salih refused to allow himself to be exploited in this way. True, he could not carry on working here and would have to return to his country, but that was more honourable than staying and indulging his partner's greed. He summoned us to say he was going home to start over, with no partner to take half the rewards for his labour. The rest of us could stay or leave. If we stayed, we would still enjoy some of the benefits he had provided but lose others, such as our rent that he had been paying. But for now at least, we wouldn't have to find new jobs, and I wouldn't have to hide from the inspectors for fear they discovered I was working illegally. My work permit, which was still with Kumar Kapoor along with my passport, had expired after I ran away and left everything behind. What love or dream can you expect from an illegal immigrant, Houria?

What a farce! I had thought of saving a place in my heart for joy. I want to be happy, to learn to laugh like I learned to talk thirty years ago, to chuckle at a silly joke or funny film, to remember—without weeping. I don't know if I can, but I will do my best to laugh each time you pass by my heart without greeting it, or you snub it and walk on. Maybe I will smile as I do now, this naive grin that twists my left lip upwards and makes me look foolish. It pains me, but it is called a smile, and I will learn to love it. I will make my peace with it, or at least conclude a truce, so it appears on my lips when I want to cry but cannot. I had resolved not to fill that place in my heart with weeping—the place you left empty, that you had filled since I first met you.

Hajj Salih pulled me aside. "Your situation is really difficult, Mukhtar. Without a passport or work permit, you have no choice," he said earnestly. I listened to him with the bitter derision I was used to suppressing for fear someone would think I meant it for them, not myself. "You have to stay, Mukhtar," he continued, "and accept what's ahead. I hate to abandon you, but I'm in the same boat, and I can't do anything for you. You have to stay, because leaving will get you into a world of trouble, and God knows where it may end." He spoke a lot, with great affection, before he left me with nothing and nobody to help me face a decision I had not made, to which I succumbed with a curious inertia.

Your messages have been blinking on my phone for nearly an hour and a half. I look over at my roommates. Midnight has fallen on their tangled desires. I imagine them waking from their long slumber and beginning to rave. Each lights his candle alone, waiting for someone to help blow it out, but no one comes. The night yawns and falls asleep, but no one comes. They write letters and poems and charms; one by one, they send their wishes and prayers heavenward, but no one comes, no one answers.

As they lie there sunk in solitude, I address them:

"May you wake to a lover knocking on the door of your cold rooms, a lover who rises after midnight from his long sleep and whispers his prayers to the highest heaven, hoping God will send him a beloved with the angels who come to rouse him for the dawn prayer."

"As for me, I want a night of joy that never ends. I want to ignite candles and wishes, not blow them out. I want to tear my heart from my breast and wash it seven times in your love to cleanse its troubles. I want the dawn moon; I want the stars to dance on the sky's cheeks as if I were in a wedding filled with cheers and trills of joy. I want a night that goes on and on, but not like this one; I want a night free of exile, sadness, and brokenness."

I pick up my phone, sensing your warmth and the perfume wafting from your words.

Houria

I have been infatuated with you ever since you taught me how to split myself into a thousand madwomen, how to hide the warmth of your hands in my fingers whenever someone tries to clasp them in a greeting, how to write to you when I need to see you, how to listen to the sea when I miss your voice. You are the man from the pages of my adolescent diary. That is how I hid you inside my heart. You are etched like wishes into my eyes; you sleep on my soul like a new dawn, leaving no room in my memory for anyone else. You are the first, the last, the only one in the chronicle of my days. When I call you "my love," sugar melts on my lips and I smile.

I love you. Do not ask me how or why, where or when. All I remember is waking one day with an insane desire to embrace you forever. I ran to open the window—perhaps your scent had inadvertently woken me. The sun was not yet up; I looked at the clock and saw it was almost four. There was no message from you on my phone to explain this spasm of longing, which tore through me like a summer storm, leaving behind a wake of destruction for all to see. That was me.

At breakfast, my father would ask why I was so distracted. I would often knock on your family's door in a panic, stammering as I asked your mother whether she had heard from you. She would say she was sorry, but she had not heard from you for two days and ask: "Why, my dear? Is something wrong?" Shaking my head and trying to muster a smile, I would reply: "No, nothing's wrong; I'm just checking. See you later, Auntie; I'm very late for work," then dash down the stairs before I had to improvise any more fibs. This morning, a colleague at the office observed that my usually pale cheeks were flushed. Had she realized I was pining for you? Why else would she ask: "Are you in love, Houria?" I retreated to the toilet to cry, the one place no one would interrupt me or intrude upon my sadness and yearning.

This love could have turned out so differently. It could have been like the stories of a small child, who tells you he adores you and you are as sweet as the candy you brought him on a quick visit. It could have been like the damp trace of his kiss on your cheek; though you reach out to wipe it off, you quickly change your mind, for some love cannot be wiped away. It could have been like your exhilaration when you pick the child up and whirl him around, as he laughs with delight and you are overcome with dizziness. He insists you carry him on your shoulders so he can touch the clouds; maybe they will rain in his hands. You refuse but later regret it, since it would have been worth the effort.

Ah, if only this love had come to fruition! That child would have grown; he would be three now, perhaps. But you keep on punishing me. Why me, and for what? For the fact that you gave up and ran away after the first time I rejected you? Did you sit yourself down and ask: "Why would she say that? Did she really mean I don't deserve her? Do I mean no more to her than the childhood sweetheart she grew up with, in whose eyes she saw her femininity blossom, a rosebud only he was allowed to pick?" It was he who had tended that bud since he first saw her crying through the neighbours' open door—a little girl mourning for the mother who had died before she could finish fastening the maroon buttons of her daughter's pink dress. It was his hand—your hand—that took her mother's place.

What gave you the right to object and storm out when I still don't know if you really love me or if your love is part of our past, like our childhood or our adolescence, scattered between a multitude of stories and desires and wishes? Why didn't you give me a second chance? Didn't I deserve that? Fine, I didn't. But the love you keep talking about; doesn't it deserve another chance?

Mukhtar

I honestly cannot answer your questions. I want to forget, but I cannot. I want to come back, and I cannot. I am split in two, and neither part has the power to banish the other and impose itself, taking me and moving on.

Hajj Salih left, and we remained behind. All of us stayed, those who had a choice and those who did not, our souls dragging their load of pain and humiliation behind them and carrying on.

Drawing on everything I had learned in the Faculty of Architecture, I built a wall around my memory, designing it without doors or windows so you could not look down on me from above. Since I was now an overnight expert in construction as well as agriculture, I put a concrete roof on top, desperately hoping my memory would die inside its prison, but it managed to escape.

Our memories do not believe in dying. They remained alive, each day drilling holes through which the smell of yesterday penetrated until I choked on it. And, as I was about to die, the new owner of the business (or rather, the old owner, since he had been one of the original partners) opened the door, and the present seeped into my chest. I inhaled it, its aroma filling my lungs, and my life was restored—or so I thought.

Chapter Twelve

The Date Farm

Houria's plea

One day we will return to dust, and from our bodies flowers and thorns will grow.

Houria

The pain I feel isn't visible to others. Am I really in pain? Something within me is expanding, choking me. Do I have the right to punish myself for disappointing you and abandoning you to an unforgiving exile? What punishment would be merciless enough for me?

You are angry with me, I know. I apologize for disturbing you now, but I wanted to tell you that yesterday, when I was about to collapse from a sudden asthma attack, I reached out for your hand, and when I felt my body was too weak to hold up my head, I begged fate for your chest to catch it. You don't realize that the ultimate weakness is stretching your hands out to clutch the air and bring it back to your lungs all at once, in the hope that it will relieve the attack. But instead, the oxygen suddenly vanishes, as if you are in a bottomless, turbulent sea. Your only choice is drowning, so you shut your eyes and yield to your fate.

I closed my eyes, delivering myself to your embrace, and when I awoke, it was as if God had banished me. You were not there; my pain had not brought you, and my ragged breathing had not returned to normal. I was like a piece of cloth whose owner, tired of patching it, leaves it to fray. My body is weak and spent, as brittle as that of a child who finds herself alone beside the sea. She plays with it a while before remembering that it is not like the one she loves; one day it may laugh and swallow her up. She tries to run away, but the sea stretches on and on and her feet are too small to leap over it.

I crumple and almost fall. And whenever my weakness and fear grow, I picture my loved ones and pull myself together. When I am on the verge of collapse, your face looks down on me from a high window, like a wish or a merciful god, and you reach out to offer me something like life.

Asthma attacks carry the smell of death. I often see it approaching my bed, but just as I am about to hand my soul over to it, I wake to the sound of your voice knocking on my door. I rush to open it, but it is only the wind disrupting the darkness, roiling its tranquillity. I curl up but I cannot cry. The bed is wide, too big to enfold me when I am frightened. I stay shivering until morning. Sometimes I look into the darkness, sometimes I address myself to the emptiness, and sometimes you give me a reproachful look and I silently lower my head.

Did you really knock on my door? Was I slow to answer, so you stormed off? Are you watching me from behind the wind? Am I still your heart, suspended between earth and sky, or have I finally fallen, and you've borne me to my eternal rest? Have you actually done that, and this pain coursing through my body like poison is just a blast from the hell of separation?

I am suffocating on myself, on my voice that is hoarse with longing, on you, who are closer than my jugular and further than a distant roar. I am suffocating on our unfinished story, our unexpected ending, on all of it.

Mukhtar

What now? Should I thank God you are safe and well? Or should I rebuke my heart for not feeling the sting of your pain or trembling with alarm as it pictures you huddled behind your oxygen mask, overcome by your weakness and your memory of me? Have you forgotten how the path shook beneath my feet the day you chased your shadow? Or how I choked on my words, unable to call out to you, and you dared not look back lest a woeful torment descend on you? You talk about illness, but you forget the man you discarded as fit only to run away, who cannot sleep a night undisturbed by yet another miserable journey.

Sometimes it happens that every cell in your body hurts, but most of all your heart, which cannot raise its voice and hands to defend itself. For so long this heart was a child who slept in your arms. How often I reproached it, shaking its shoulder to get its attention or splashing it with cold water in the vain hope it would wake. This rebellious heart will kill me!

How can you demand my forgiveness when you abandoned me to the darkness, to be tossed unmercifully among its nights? This is your favourite pastime—subjugating me to your heart whenever you want. I always followed you like your shadow, but it is time for this shadow to break free; it is time I asked God to grant my soul peace before it departs with all its torment. It is time to shout: peace be upon me, not upon you—not upon the hurt, longing, and tears, or the exile and suffering. Peace be upon me and me alone, not upon all your memories, whims, and caprices, or any of those who inhabited your heart or collapsed into your arms.

Don't send your messages; please stop. I am the one who is tired, who cannot stand it any longer. Your messages bring only intolerable pain, reopening unhealed wounds, burning me, but all I can do is wait for them. Sometimes they are bittersweet, fuelling my insomnia, and I smile as if my soul had suddenly been restored. Other times they arrive—fair, or unfair, they come like life and death—and I am weak; I can only wait.

Nothing stays the same. Every road that once joined us has led to an absence devoid of all but our footprints, their traces eroded and effaced by forgetfulness. We've even thought of donating our conversations to the first passing caravan; perhaps it can sell our words for a pittance to some lonesome fellow to fill his ever-growing solitude.

The days pass, but not as we wish. They are cold, empty of any warmth to which our sleeping desires could awake, as if—like this rainy night with its heavy, smothering clouds—we were not made for love. Why don't I long to go outside like I used to and chase the rain, racing to catch each drop with my hand or my tongue or kicking it as I pictured it flying straight into the net in my best goal ever? I pull the blanket tighter and hide from the drumming of the rain on the ground, fearful a bolt of lightning may tear me from the earth. Sleep evades me. I try to seduce it with my closed eyes and my hands, tucked between my legs in an effort to shelter from everything I fear in this land that is so far from my childhood, from my mother, from your eyes.

I was not always afraid of rain. I once believed it brought life in one hand and joy in the other. But the rain here is different; it brings death in one hand and sorrow in the other. When it rains, people die, and even trees cannot survive. The last deluge carried off a man, his wife, and their three daughters, the oldest no more than seven. The wadi washed them away in its torrent; it disgorged the man alive but swallowed his wife and daughters, handing them over to death. That was how the man emerged empty-handed from a marriage of more than eight years, deprived of a kind and loving wife and three daughters who once danced around him like butterflies. They all died and left him to gnaw on his sorrow and loneliness.

Will the father endure a living death, I wonder? Or will he forget and remarry a year later, siring new children? Out of loyalty, he may name their first daughter after his late wife, or he may not. As for the dead, they will remain far away, waiting for the rain to end, and the girls will stop dancing to the rhythm of the raindrops. Their hands will no longer stretch toward an approaching cloud as they shriek delightedly: "Abi! It's going to rain!"

"The Lord giveth and the Lord taketh away." So I try to soothe my heart as it aches for you. When you withdrew from me, I believed that prayers were only for the faithful, and mine had not been sincere enough for God to accept them—or so I thought. I stopped praying and set out on an uncharted path, abandoning my piety to an unknown future, turning away from God, my faith in Him, and all the blessings He bestows on me without my realising. And now here I am, rejected by the cosmos. I am surrounded by the four points of the compass, plus the sky and the mute earth that joins clay to clay—the clay of our bodies to the clay of the grave. The earth takes us to nourish its trees. We may become a flower, or we may re-emerge in the cells of a thorn, but for the most part, we do not choose how our souls will be reborn: as a flower or as a thorn. Nor does it matter as much as we believe.

I am wondering what to do today. It is Friday, the day to take a break from work and enjoy time with friends or read a book I have downloaded instead of wasting money on an expensive hard copy, since I should be saving up. How ironic—it reminds me of how I once hoarded my school allowance to buy a magazine or book recommended by a friend or teacher. Now books have become a waste of money.

The telephone rouses me from my indecision. Maybe it is a friend wanting to go out and enjoy our free time, but no, it is a message from you. I pick up the phone, shivering with pleasure as some dreams awake and others depart. My whole body starts to perspire, especially my hand. It hasn't stopped sweating since it first touched you, a baby only a few hours old, when I went with my mother to offer congratulations on your birth. She asked God to make you a virtuous daughter, to give you the affection your mother had taken away when she went to meet her Maker after haemorrhaging to death during an obstructed labour. I hastily dry my damp palm on my leg so I can open your message. It is different from your other messages. I don't let my surprise distract me but yield to the pleasant tingling that runs through me upon opening it.

Houria

I am a rebellious woman. You know I'm different from other women—I wasn't created to hide behind a tent of silk. I always dreamt I would snatch my voice from the silence of earth's women, that I would scream at death for taking my mother when she gave birth to me. Everyone consoles me by saying she granted me her beauty and her life, but their eyes say: 'If only she had taken that beauty and life with her.'

Why do you blame me for fearing poverty? Wasn't it poverty that snatched away my mother when my father couldn't afford for her to deliver me in a private hospital? Didn't that same poverty suddenly fill up all the beds in the government hospital and drive my mother outside to give birth, the agony of obstructed labour gradually stripping away her life?

I want to wrap myself in life. Why did you make light of my fear that death would take me as it had my mother, with our first child, ripping my life away and giving it to the child? Our child, whom we'll watch growing, moving inside me day after day, as we imagine its every detail and visit the gynaecologist to learn if it is a girl or a boy. If it is a girl, I'll be sad, because she'll carry my fate and that of my mother. I'll cry, but you'll tell me everything is going to be fine. I won't be convinced; I'll continue to be anxious, waking up whenever the spectre of death comes rushing to take me away, each peaceful night ending in anxiety and tears.

You don't understand because you don't want to. You flung your dream in front of me and made no move to pick it up. Yes, I wronged you, but you were party to my crime. Neither of us was strong enough to hold onto the other. And now here we are, both of us losers—weeping together, dying together—and though I have admitted I was wrong, you will not.

Why did you disdain a woman like me and abandon her? You are a coward; like all men in love, you want a ripe apple you can bite into whenever you wish, with no sense of sin great or small, no fear of expulsion from paradise.

How I would like to drift off to sleep without your face looking down on me, filling the vast spaces between us, without my fingers roving compulsively across the apps on my phone, round and round, the way I used to spin the globe in the classroom as I searched for a map that resembled my country, not finding it, not finding you.

I let my fingers finish their circling, and I travel to a place where I cannot be with you. But you won't release me. Wherever I go, you cling to my hand like a child afraid of getting lost. Why do you resist your heart? How did you become so cruel? Am I not your beloved, the little girl you took under your wing from the day she was born and found herself motherless, whom your mother took so she would not lack maternal love and affection?

Do you remember Om Ali, the sweet that I love? It was the only sweet your mother was good at making. I learned to love it at the age of five, when I was playing at your house and smelled it for the first time. I could not get it out of my mind, but I didn't dare ask my aunt Um Mukhtar for some; I was too bashful. I went home, closed the door of my room, and cried, asking God to resurrect my mother to make me Om Ali—the kind your mother made—and then she could die again. God sent you to knock on the door, the smell of Om Ali preceding you and rousing me from my bed. I ran to you, my face still streaked with tears.

"What's the matter?" you asked.

"Nothing. I was just asking God to send my mother back so she could make Om Ali for me."

You laughed and hugged me, whispering: "God has sent her to live in our house and make Om Ali for you there." That day, I was sure God had taken my mother from me and replaced her with your mother, who never raised her voice in anger or scolded me for my mistakes. She would not let my father punish me, but stroked my hair and told him:

"This is a motherless child. Whoever hurts her will not enter Heaven or have even a whiff of it."

You were as tender as your mother, patting my head and hugging me, a seven-year-old boy as mature as a man of seventy. I loved you; you know that. It was something that went without saying, taken for granted, like the fact that we grew older and taller each day, like the beard sprouting on your chin, which you carefully trimmed to make yourself look handsome and manly. You would point out that I needed to get rid of a few little hairs before they grew like yours and people couldn't tell us apart. I didn't get cross with you, since you were my mirror, my window onto life. And though my body was rapidly developing, I never felt shy or embarrassed around you as I might have with a brother, since you were not my brother. And so I began to love you differently, but I failed to hold on to you because I feared poverty might suddenly snatch me from you.

I rejected you because I was afraid of death. I don't want to die suddenly like my mother, but I cannot live without you. How can I make peace with myself and with you? Come back to me, Mukhtar. Forgive me for not understanding life properly. Come back as you are, without money or gifts, without sadness or exile. Come back as the beloved of whom I have not had my fill, before the roses on my chest wilt. Come back to me, and it won't matter if I die giving birth to your first child.

Mukhtar

You are silent. Yes, you are silent. This time you sent a voice message, your voice running through my veins until I felt weak. I followed the sound until it ended, my ear detecting almost every beat of your pulse. Your breathing was neither fast nor slow, but more like church bells pealing to awake someone's faith. And whenever my heart reached out drowsily from beneath the covers, I patted its head and tucked it back in. It was only the time for dreaming, not for waking early. It does not matter if I wake a little late. Perhaps something will free me from this love. Perhaps I will travel another path, one that does not lead me to you, all the times jumbled up in my mind, as if I no longer cared about anything but pursuing you, searching for you, reaching you. It is said that all paths will bring us to what we want, if we are sincere. My desire is more sincere even than a child's craving for a toy or an orphan's dream of a mother who won't return. But not all sayings are true, and I did not reach my goal. I admit it: I have lost my power to resist; I have laid down all my weapons.

Some years and a day ago—I no longer remember exactly—I made the same mistake I am thinking of making now. I closed the doors, the windows, and the curtains—no, there were no curtains, or maybe they are gone now?—heaping reproach on myself, striking my head with my hands, or my hands with my head, it doesn't matter which, since the outcome is the same. As I paced around the room, I discovered a broken floor tile, another that the ground had pushed up, and an abandoned anthill. Even ants don't like living with exiles.

I closed the door behind me. I stopped hitting my head with my hands, or vice versa, and took the stairs three at a time. It's all right to do something wrong as long as you don't hurt anyone, my soul cajoled me. And like someone who rules the world and knows he calls all the shots, I bounded down the stairs without suspecting that my look into your eyes would bring me back with my heart in tow, like a child whose mother has rebuked him for not tidying his room.

All decisions are meaningless if we dare not implement them. I came back up the stairs, as shame-faced as when Shaykh Yassin's cane met my back before my father scooped me into his arms and glared at him, departing without a word that would help the Shaykh swallow the spittle of rage on his fleshy lips. Holding back tears, you raced to the top of the stairs and slammed the door in my face. "Please don't change your mind," you whispered imploringly, like a tempest about to sweep me away. I backed away but had to place both feet on each step to control my nerves. I was tense and confused, my grip on the banister betraying how weak and fragile I was before you.

This time, too, you lose your temper, threatening to cut me off for good, to wash your hands of me as you did before.

Houria

"We must meet again, or we must forget. It is time for us to forget," you repeat, "time for this nonsense to end. One day, you will wake up and not find my voice. I won't whisper to you to awaken your heart; I might not even say goodbye. I'll be like a station you passed through; tickets won't help you and the trains won't tell you where I've gone. I'll be lost in your memory, and the road that gave us a Fairouz song and a flower will close for endless repairs. I will lose myself, efface myself, forget myself in a place even I do not know, so my heart can't disclose it to you. I know my heart won't agree to leave you, so I'll let it decide whether to follow me or stay with you. Believe me, its decision won't matter. I don't trust my heart, so I won't tell it I am leaving, lest it creep up behind me on a day that is further away than you think. I'll fold up all the years, leave them behind, and depart for good to whatever oblivion holds. I will not dangle like an apple from paradise, and no man but you will pluck me."

"I know what I want—finally, I know what I want—but it did not coincide with what you wanted, and it never will. You won't forgive my mistake, and I am tired of begging for a forgiveness that never comes. Must I die so you will ask God to forgive me? Why won't you forgive me, so I know God will?"

Mukhtar

I am drowning in your bewildered eyes. Your image appears before like an irrefutable fact. I am sure there is no escape; I have to go home. This running away will get us nowhere—we are dying far from one other.

Chapter Thirteen

The Date Farm

Mukhtar's confession

Those who return, like those who are lost, are searching for something they cannot find.

When Taj shouted at me, I nearly dropped the rope that secured me to the top of the palm tree, but I managed to catch myself before falling to my death.

"Run away from what? Where? What's happened?"

"There's no time to explain. Just get out of here!"

I scrambled down from the tree in a rush. Grabbing my belongings that Taj al-Islam had brought, I dashed off in the direction he pointed, with no idea where I was going or what awaited me there.

I ran for countless hours for no reason other than that, if I stopped, I would be jailed and deported after paying the many fines for which I had no money. I stopped to calm my ragged breathing, as its jerking told me it was fed up with me and wanted to abandon me in this godforsaken place. My heart raced as if trying to escape my chest, like a flock of birds assaulted by hunters from all sides, plummeting to earth one by one. How could I gather up my pulse as it rested its head upon the earth, begging it for a handful of dirt to slake its thirst? I collapsed on the ground, dust returning to dust—not the usual return, but one shuddering with exhaustion, oblivious to its surroundings.

I woke a while later to find the sun eating my body alive after the earth had failed to fry it and instead grilled it over an open fire, though it was neither cooked nor turned to ashes for the wind to carry away.

As I lay in a daze, I heard a sound I could not identify, like the quavering of my mother's prayers as she entreated God to preserve me and return me to her safely, ending with the words: "I commend you to God, for nothing we commend to Him is ever lost." How often had she sworn this prayer would bring me back, and that if she failed to recite it even one day, I might not return? I wonder if even now, she is reciting those same words.

Or perhaps it was the boom of my father's voice. Whenever he could not solve a problem, he would intone Surat Ya-Sin over and over. Recite, Abi, for between your son and death there is but a frayed hair, which needs only a long arm like Shaykh Yassin's to reach out and pluck it, green and fresh. I turn over slightly as Shaykh Yassin's cane flays my tender back for failing to start my day with the morning prayers. "But I haven't learnt them, Shaykh. I'll memorise them tomorrow, I promise. I'll recite them seven times, and I won't forget to blow my efforts in the Devil's face."

"You silly boy. I don't belong to you; this is just a stupid dream."

So Houria used to say, the scourge of her vanity harsher than the dance of Shaykh Yassin's cane on my back. They seemed to take turns whipping me, one flogging my back while the other lashed my chest.

"Wake up! Come on, wake up!"

I opened my eyes, but it was only a crow scratching in the dirt. Perhaps he was seeking to bury my disgrace, for, unlike Cain, he had no brother cast aside as discarded and worthless, repudiated by life and spat out of its giant mouth, as immense as the mouth of the cave the jinn had adopted as the headquarters for their chief with his buck teeth. That great opening almost disgorged me after a small jinn discovered I had entered their headquarters to escape the thing

Taj al-Islam had told me to flee before it could catch and devour me. Will it help me now to ask which is more merciful—being swallowed up or being spat out? No; after all, I am now discarded, worthless.

I closed my eyes again. I saw the bucktoothed leader of the jinn. In his left hand, he held a scythe, its gleam almost blinding me, while his right hand rested on the back of someone bowed over like an old palm branch created just for that purpose. I was surrounded by five fierce and formidable jinn who never disobeyed their leader but always did as they were commanded. Was it really five? No, I think it was eight. At first, I took these phantoms for shadows, but they seemed to be the jinn who are invisible to humans. I felt their hands attach iron rods to my body. The deep silence was broken only by the chief as he whispered to the jinn beside him, who bustled back and forth before finally coming to rest beside his leader wordlessly, as if the chief could see and hear and follow everything happening outside.

The cave was the largest I had ever seen. It was like a self-contained world or endless kingdom, distinguished from our world only by its mouth. It seemed to reach to the very top of heaven, while I was in the depths of the earth, unable to see a way to escape it. Was this the opening through which the jinn ascend to heaven to eavesdrop, chased by a fiery flame, as the Qur'an says? "Except for him who may eavesdrop, and then a bright flame pursues him." Who knows? Perhaps, or perhaps not. What do I care? I have never thought of entering heaven or eavesdropping on the angels to discover the unseen world, but in spite of that, the fates continue to kick me back and forth.

Finally, after the chief jinn beckoned mysteriously to his entourage, two of them approached me. They seized me under the arms and ascended into the air. Closing my eyes, I found myself rising at a speed beyond my human grasp. Suddenly everything appeared tiny except for the chief, who grew larger and larger the further we rose. They lifted me out of that cavernous maw until the earth was no longer visible. And the sky? There was no sky—only endless space. They abruptly released me, and I dropped to the ground like a hawk overtaken by death as it soars in the skies. It plummets toward the ground, oblivious to how the earth will receive it or what end awaits, never thinking its life will no longer bloom in the sky like an eternal star.

Cold water is dripping on my face. I appear to have passed through my limbo and entered paradise, since this ice-cold water doesn't belong to the desert. Were the last three months enough to cancel out all my sins? Did they render me as blameless as the day my mother bore me, allowing me to enter paradise with no reckoning or punishment for all my years of falling short? After all, my mother used to whisper to me that God's mercy is closer than His anger, and a single tear can erase the sins of a lifetime, no matter how long. I wonder, are these the same tears I shed when I first entered the village mosque?

I feel the cold water on my face again and open my eyes. It is the same desert. I look around, but there is no sign of paradise. I am certainly not in hell, where there is only scalding water to drink, so what is this cold water? Is it zamharir, the icy depths of hell? I doubt it, since I don't feel cold. Hell is still beneath me. I must be one of the Dwellers on the Heights, who stand midway between paradise and Hell. The fire licking me from below and the cold water dripping on me from paradise are helping me endure my situation. So my good deeds and my sins have balanced out. Thank God! This is far better than spending eternity in Hell, eating thorns and pus and drinking boiling water.

I turn toward the cool and peaceful hand that has reached out to touch my face, and, as if the moon had split open, a visage appears. I close my eyes for a moment, finally convinced I am in fact in paradise, and this is the face of an angel created from light. His hand returns to rest quietly on my face, and I turn my wandering gaze toward him. His worried smile exudes a compassion that reaches from here to Judgment Day. Lifting my head with one hand, with the other he gives me a drink of water so refreshing I will never feel thirst again. The intoxication of life returns to my veins and my blood expands as that luminous face slips into my soul. I reach my hand up to touch it and am surprised by how rough it is. So I am not in paradise after all, since the people there don't have coarse skins, as far as I know. And before my thoughts carry me away, his voice rolls over me, as sonorous as the Psalms of David.

"Nobody lives around here. How did you get here?"

I try to answer, but a weight in my head has gripped my tongue. I let my head slide from his hand and follow the pull of gravity. I lack the strength to resist both the earth and its creatures. My gaze wanders through the unending space in search of a shadow where I can take shelter and escape my frailty before it kills me.

"No one comes here but me," the man continued warily. "I hunt for the hives of rare wild bees and extract their honey, since as God says in Surat al-Nahl, 'there is healing for people' in it. I roam through the mountains for days without returning home. When I first saw you, I wasn't sure if you were human, but when I recited protective verses from the Qur'an and you didn't run away, I was reassured. Now tell me honestly: who are you running away from?"

I rummaged through my childhood memories for a white lie he might believe. He watched me, his eyes navigating my bloodstream like an expert skipper firmly gripping the sea's tiller, until I gave up searching in my toybox. Its mahogany colour used to fade every time my small hand tossed a new adventure or tall tale inside it. How terrified I was of being exposed after the box had overflowed with all those stories, and they began climbing the walls of my small room, transforming it into a world where I reigned supreme—the knight, the swaggering hero, king of the castle. The box resembled a small coffin, though the memories it held neither died nor eroded but stayed alive, competing with one another to dominate my memory. If one didn't triumph, it would turn on its fellows. Each murdered story left behind it a host of details which regenerated to fill the empty space in my memory.

"I have no idea. I ran away because Taj al-Islam told me to."

The man shook his head indignantly.

"It seems that Taj al-Islam sacrifices one man a year."

I look at him, imploring him not to spoil my image of a man whom I had believed to be so far above the rest of us that life bows down and tries to please them. My eyes trembled as, from time to time, my lashes tried to reassure them. But the man continued:

"This is the third year in a row I've found somebody on the run for no reason except that Taj al-Islam chased him away and he couldn't find his way back to the farm."

I looked behind me. How had I ended up here? Had I run in a single direction, or had I taken care to cover my tracks, backtracking to confuse any would-be pursuer? I shook my head violently, trying to dispel these thoughts. Taj al-Islam, the man who had reached out his hand to me as my lungs filled with the smell of dirt during a prostration so lengthy he thought I had died? Taj al-Islam, who told me afterward that my face bore the unmistakeable mark of true repentance? What had he seen—someone repentant or someone gullible? Those who return, like those who are lost, are searching for something they cannot find. I remembered that I had been paid only the day before I ran away. Was that really yesterday, or was another life entwined with mine, the two so jumbled up I no longer knew what day it was?

As if a snake had bitten me in my sleep, I leapt to my feet and began rooting through the belongings Taj had brought. There was no sign of the two months' salary that Shaykh Sulayman, with great affection, had insisted on paying me after I had asked him to set aside my pay for two months. Nor did I find the extra amounts he had given me when I told him I was doing something for the first time. Shaykh Sulayman had been thrilled when I confessed I had never worked as a farmer and praised my candour.

I remembered how Taj al-Islam had once volunteered to deliver my wages to me, but Am Sulayman said he preferred to hand them to me himself, since it warmed his heart to see our eyes light up with these small pleasures. I recalled Am Sulayman once telling me that honesty is more beautiful than the lies with which we delude ourselves to make others think more highly of us. Eyes that do not love us as we are—with all our faults and shortcomings—do not deserve to see us, so why should we beautify ourselves for them?

Am Sulayman used to roar with laughter as he watched me open the traps Taj al-Islam had set for birds or shoo away the birds lured by greed or curiosity. He was surprised to see me scatter grain far from the snares Taj al-Islam had put out to secure his supper. Taj was equally astonished to find the traps empty of food to blunt his evening hunger and save him the expense of eating in the local restaurant. Before my arrival, he had been accustomed to trapping his supper easily. I told him that the birds had wised up to his tricks. After all, even birds can learn. It is only man who does not benefit from the experience of others. He must try everything to learn, but most of the time he just repeats the same mistakes.

When Am Sulayman asked me what I was doing, I told him I was trying to atone for my past sins against these small flying creatures. As a boy, I had been so skilled at hunting them that I could dismember them with a single shot. I would return late in the evening, hauling the victims of my little slingshot, their wings still floating in the air, as I strutted like a warrior fresh from victory, his enemies littering the battlefield or lashed with rope to his strong hands. I have no idea how I had acquired the skill and strength to make even the shrewdest bird fall stone-dead into my hands.

I did not forget to confess another of my secrets to Am Sulayman in my attempt to expiate the crimes that had burdened me since childhood. As a child, I used to save some of my pocket money for a pigeon, then delightedly release it into the sky as I attempted in vain to forget the bodies that used to fall into my hands one after another. I hoped the pigeon would find some of the wings detached from the corpses of my victims and ask them to forgive me. Then I could replace their image with one of the bodies rising rather than falling. No such luck; it looks like I will not forget those falling bodies until I see my own body rise and fly before it drops to the ground: alone, lifeless, and friendless.

The Bedouin placed his hand on my shoulder, bringing me back to the present.

"Don't let anyone take the rewards for your labour. Get up; go back where you were working. Find Taj al-Islam and take back what he stole from you."

I tried to stand, but my feet would not cooperate. He reached out to help me up. In the noonday sun, my shadow was almost invisible, a reminder of how puny and powerless I was. It clung to my feet fearfully, peeking out just enough to record its presence beside me at this moment of crisis.

The Bedouin seemed to understand my unease. He traced the outline of my shadow in the dirt, then pushed me slightly to one side. The lines in the dirt did not move. "You see? Even our small shadows won't allow themselves to be scarred. Go freely, healed of all your wounds, and don't allow anyone to scar your soul."

We parted after he had escorted me to the road that would lead me back, or to a fresh start. I laid out my belongings. They were the ones I had arrived with, only a few garments to cover myself so I would not be naked in both body and soul. I surveyed the road, debating whether I should return to reclaim the rewards of my labour from Taj al-Islam, or forget them and find a safe haven for the vulnerable like me. The sun was about to set. I had to decide quickly or find shelter before night came and I found myself completely alone.

I picked up my things and left. Behind me, the sun waved, asking me to come back, or perhaps bidding me farewell. Who was I that the sun should ask me to return with the dawn? And what would my presence or absence change in this expanding universe? Would the cosmic order be changed by one man's fall or another's rise? Certainly not. I turned toward the sun and waved, mustering from my exhaustion a smile that went on and on like an old song of which people never tire.

Do you remember how you adored the songs of Abdul Haleem Hafez, especially "Like the Air"? Were you hinting that you were like air—impossible to grasp, to live on or without? Though I can sense you, I cannot touch or see you; I cannot fill my palms with you the way I fill my lungs. Were you really generous like the air that entered my soul to keep it alive? Or was the only resemblance that your approach brought life and your departure took it away? Why did you always hum this song and laugh when you reached the verse that went:

"I threw away the rose, and I blew out the candle, my love."

Were you thinking of me as I flung my heart down for you to crush with your high heel before leaving, after you enjoyed watching it grovel in the dirt, unable to escape you or seek refuge with you?

Why, when you claim I mean nothing to you, do you do your utmost to increase my love for you, to strengthen our bond? What vanity is this; what kind of egotism lives inside you? Why do I now see you so filled with conceit, enjoying my pain and mocking my tears, while hearts throw themselves beneath your feet? What soul crouches between your ribs like a lioness, snarling at anyone who tries to approach?

I remember the last Eid I spent with you. On the eve of the feast, you asked me: "How will I look tomorrow?"

I was about to say you would be stunning, but you spoke first:

"I'll be beautiful, won't I?"

Then you gazed at me, your eyes aglow with a vanity I mistook for love, and I smiled.

"Of course you'll be gorgeous. Who would dare say otherwise? You know no other woman is as beautiful. You're unique."

You smiled, and everything smiled with you: my heart and my soul, the earth and the sky, the trees, the birds and the Nile, which slept contentedly that night as if rocking between two moons.

Every footstep took me further from the sun and closer to the darkness, as I quickened my steps in hopes of finding a place for myself on the earth across which I was racing.

Chapter Fourteen

The Date Farm

Exposing treachery

Memory is a gateway that cannot be closed, for it is always pierced with holes to the soul.

Houria

I am attached to you, as if you were part of me or created from me, as if you were life itself. I love you so much it has made me ill, as if I had just learned I have a terminal disease but smile, knowing that I will live—and die—with you. Together we will breathe and suffer; together we will rest between bouts of pain. Even when I lose consciousness, you will be with me. Do you know what that means? It means I can't escape from you or you from me.

Nonetheless, this distance is killing me, like a knife that continues cutting the cord that once bound us. Though that cord was not made of gossamer, it did not hold. I know I was the one who reached out to tear it. What a fool I was! I did not know what I wanted; I admit I neither knew nor understood what I was doing. I thought I was pursuing my happiness, my dreams and desires, until one day I tripped over them, and for once, your hand was not there to catch me. I searched for it everywhere, like the mother who lost her child during the great pilgrimage, when the crowd swept him away before she realised she had dropped his hand, and who hunted for him ever after. Like her, I am still searching for you, and neither of us can find what we've lost.

Imagine that the distance now dividing our bodies will one day separate our hearts and souls. Count with me: how many flowers will wilt and how many birds lose their wings? How many nights will not be followed by dawn? How many lives will end while they were storing up their laughter for the morrow?

I love you. If only you could believe that all will be well, as long as this heart lives with you and presses you into the candies it gives to children, hoping that when they grow up, they will fill the earth with peace and love. If you would give me but one chance to say it, to let my eyes complete the sentence we did not finish—perhaps because we did not start it as we should have. Read it in my eyes just once, and if you don't believe me, you can leave again. And if you do believe me, then plant an olive tree in the courtyard of our house, a tree from neither East nor West that will glow when we water it, its oil lighting up minarets, churches, and temples so that lovers and the blind may be guided to them, and don't leave—never, ever leave—without my hand in yours.

Mukhtar

I don't know how many times I have read your message; I have lost count in my quest to forget. But I did not forget. My heart forsook me and chose to remain with you. Where can I hide my face from sadness? How can I stop my lips from trembling at the mention of your name, when you have left no part of my heart unscathed?

For five years, whenever you passed through my thoughts—like a rock I tripped over, a night that disowned its moon, or a wave that crashed over me as I rode in a rubber raft, having surrendered to a shivering dark—it was only you who appeared to me beneath every crease in my palm and every breeze that entered my chest, only you to whom I chanted my spells, breathing your name into every word until they brought you back to me. If you only knew how hard I find this voluntary separation, how hard it is to draw the distances and race across them without stopping before I flag down the first train, which stops to pick me up before it continues on its way. Though I wish it would stop again, it does not, hurtling along the endless roads without ever arriving, going so fast that places seem to be leaving it rather than it leaving them, neither knowing nor remembering one other.

I look around. I am the only passenger on this moving train. Where is it taking me? I have no idea. The one thing I know, and profoundly regret, is that I chose to board it. I did not know it would take me back to you, that you would not cross my breast except to enter my soul. I had no idea that endings are only other beginnings, harsher and more painful. I did not realise departure is a gateway that cannot be closed for good. It is always pierced with holes through which memory filters, like a light that a man drowning in darkness cannot ignore.

Or perhaps it's more like the glint of the gold that fills so many of the nearby shops. Most of their customers are Omani, but one glance at their proprietors' faces tells you they are not. The proprietors wear national dress, but when you speak with them, their accent will erase any doubt. In no way does their accent resemble Arabic, though they affect to be Arab, specifically Omani. I believe some have been granted citizenship in appreciation for the many years they have lived here—working, striving, and building, putting the country's interests before their own and before their overflowing bank accounts, with which the local and international banks are filled to bursting. Excuse me, I mean their accounts that never grow, that are—as everyone is absolutely sure—completely empty.

My friend laughs when I play this broken record, as he calls it, though I retort that it's not broken, even if no one is listening and I'm like a man who talks to himself, my only audience a friend who laughs hysterically whenever he hears this refrain. I can't understand how these people own and control the gold shops. "I've never once seen an Omani standing behind those glass cases draped in gold jewellery," one of them told me. A friend of mine, he is forever mocking my "radical" ideas, though I'm not sure if by radical, he means revolutionary—a word we hear all the time and which, as we've seen, only results in death, destruction, and the dismemberment of countries—or if he means bullshit.

Things were completely different in Nizwa. There, Omanis owned all the shops, as I saw after Hajj Salih sent me there to manage a new branch of his juice business before he decided to depart Oman for good. The new owner fired me rather than take the risk of employing an illegal worker. He offered me a choice—leave or be handed over to authorities—so I chose to leave.

At first, I had no idea where to go. But I had developed a stronger backbone, and it pointed me toward the village I had fled, though I had done nothing wrong. I needed to understand what had happened: to confront Taj al-Islam and expose his wrongdoing to Am Sulayman. After considerable effort, I reached the village. I had never thought I would return or be able to find it, even if I tried. But determination works miracles, and I made it there.

When I arrived at the farm, I found Am Sulayman in his usual position, sitting on a palm mat and leaning against the trunk of an ancient Christ's-thorn tree. As the ants marched over his leg, the birds pecked up their daily share of the grain he tossed them or savoured the berries fallen from the tree. Before Am Sulayman could react, I greeted him, bending over to kiss his head and his hand as his sons did. He gazed at me in disbelief, as if he had never expected to see me again. Ignoring the ants, he sprang to his feet and stared at me thunderstruck. Placing his hands on my shoulders, he squeezed my arms from shoulder to fingertips as if reassuring himself I was real.

"Why did you run away?" he asked, turning away, his face sad and reproachful. Choking up more than once, I began telling him what I had been through and the treachery I had fallen victim to. Showing neither anger nor acceptance, he merely listened without reacting. Confused by his silence, I asked him:

"Am Sulayman, can you hear me?"

"Come with me."

Taking my hand, he pulled me along like a child until we reached the room Taj al-Islam and I had once shared.

"Two weeks after you suddenly disappeared, when Taj al-Islam was out cutting alfalfa for the livestock, someone broke into his room and stole everything. Taj went berserk. We took him to several hospitals, and they all agreed he had suffered a nervous breakdown. As you can see, he is no longer in his right mind. He talks to himself constantly and doesn't respond to anyone. If you bring him food, he will eat, but if you don't, he will go hungry and thirsty without complaint.

"I had planned to send him home, but he refused to go. The first time I reserved a seat on a plane for him, I also reserved a seat for one of his friends, to be sure Taj made it back to his family. But he slipped away from us in the airport and came back to his room. We looked high and low before we found him here in this condition. Some time later, I made another reservation for him and two companions who could follow him every step of the way, but we couldn't even get him into the airport taxi. I finally gave up and let him stay here, but I'm afraid something bad will happen to him while he's in this state. God is just, my son; He is just. He is punishing Taj for what he did to you."

He turned to me.

"But tell me about yourself. What have you been doing these last few months? Do you have a job? Where? Are you happy there? Are they paying you a decent wage? Is anyone bothering you? Did you miss me?"

Am Sulayman continued peppering me with questions without waiting for my answers. When he had tired of talking, he fell silent. When I finally stopped smiling, I told him I had been working for Hajj Salih, but the new owner of the business had fired me because

I was here illegally. Am Sulayman told me how deeply he deeply regretted my situation and the fact that I had run away. If I hadn't left, he added, he would have put me in charge of running the farm, but now, someone else had taken Taj al-Islam's place. Am Sulayman promised he would find me work and would not let me leave again until he knew where I was going and could guarantee I would not face more hard times.

Now I find myself in the heart of the capital, in the bewitching seaside suburb of Muttrah, holding a letter of recommendation from Am Sulayman. The port stretches outward like a night of farewell, and anchored ships stand like sentinels, enlivening the nights of the drowsy sea before them. Mountains encircle the city like a protective cordon, flanked by al-Jalali and al-Mirani, the two citadels the Portuguese built as their garrison when they occupied Oman. A friend of mine claims that beneath the waters of the Gulf is a tunnel connecting the two forts. Did the sea bring foreigners to settle in this city and make it a centre for the gold trade? Is this the only place in the country that foreigners control, or do they control other cities and trades?

Many are the stories the local shop-owners tell about the hammour—the big fish, as they've nicknamed the important merchants here—though I think they're just whales that have swallowed everything in their path—hammour, sardines, and people—before breaking through the water's surface and ascending to the sky. What hammour are they talking about, my friend and the naive souls like him? Real hammour don't eat humans, while these have gobbled up the earth and everything on it, leaving nothing in their wake.

"Why are you so angry, Mukhtar, as if this were your land and your country, and it's you they have robbed? These people were here long before you, my friend. In this country, you're just a vagabond and a foreigner. One day, you'll have to go back to your country, and on that day, you'll forget every memory you have of this place."

My friend doesn't know that another year of my life elapsed today, joining all the other years weighed down with disappointment. I have nothing to show for it but one less year in my life. My friend thinks I can forget the time I have wasted here. He doesn't know that I dawdled in front of the mirror this morning, folding up my thirty-first year and shelving it with the rest of my memories, to be forgotten one day. I counted the white hairs encroaching on my jet-black hair, competing to see which of them can bring my youth to an early end. This is the first time I have befriended the mirror and asked it to be honest with me, to help me count what I cannot count myself. I stand there, unable to answer the question bedevilling me: why do exiles turn grey prematurely?

Slicking down my unruly hair with that question, I put on the clothes Shaykh Mansur gave me. They once belonged to a man six years younger than me, who departed this life during his final year of medical school, six months after I began working for his father. I am so thin now that the clothes hang off me, as if to say: "We don't belong to you," just as Houria said to me five years ago. The words have the same effect as hers, though people are not the same as things. Nonetheless, to humour Shaykh Mansur, I wear his son's clothing. If my mother knew, she would die of shame. From my childhood until the moment I arrived in Oman, I had worn only brand-new clothes.

Sometimes everything feels wonderful, almost as if you are in paradise, and then you stumble over an immense sorrow that rips your heart from your chest. We never know where death is going to strike next. So it happened that Shaykh Mansur collapsed from shock when he heard that his son had met an untimely death. The son, about to graduate with honours from medical school, was his family's pride, hope, and joy, the doctor who was going to treat everyone, from the foreigner to the youngest child in the family. Suddenly, he became helpless, and even the medical profession could offer his family no hope for his treatment or survival. The loss would leave a lasting mark on the father. He had placed his greatest hopes in his son the doctor. Whenever the young man arrived in his white coat, Shaykh Mansur would lean back in his comfortable chair with a contented smile and summon us:

"The doctor's arrived. Come and greet him."

His shock at his son's illness, which was discovered in its late stages, was even greater than his pride in the young man. When he heard his son had collapsed at the university and was now in a coma, Shaykh Mansur was at an utter loss. The tests revealed that the young man's brain cancer had led to complete and irreversible organ failure. The son's concern for his father had been too great to tell him of the blinding headaches that nearly made him pass out. Instead, he had secluded himself in his room, dosing himself with antacids and painkillers until, after a long night of insomnia and intolerable pain, sleep eventually came. In the morning, he would rouse himself and accompany his father to the mosque to share the rewards of dawn prayer. So that his father could not see how thin he had grown, he doubled his food intake, and whenever his stomach protested, he would vomit up what he had forced into it.

The father learned all this afterwards from the sole friend in whom his son had confided about his splitting headaches after making him swear—by God and everyone he cherished—not to tell anyone, lest the news reach his father and upset him. The young man refused any diagnostic tests for fear his father would discover the results and go out of his mind with worry, which his son could not bear. The son lay brain-dead for three weeks, long enough for his father to resign himself to disconnecting the life-support machines. It was left to the doctors to cover the son's face with the white cloth both son and father had so long dreamt of, although the two whites could not have been more different.

Shaykh Mansur was a worthy man, kind and generous, and his son's death only increased his generosity. I became his son, and, through him, my father came back to life. How could it have been otherwise, when Am Sulayman had entrusted me to him? The only difference was that I was no longer young. I no longer climbed on my father's shoulders to touch the sky or see the houses of the faithful in paradise; I no longer cried when I felt weak, as Abi dried my tears and said sternly:

"Men don't cry, Mukhtar, and you're a man."

I no longer cry, Abi. I am afraid that if I do, Shaykh Mansur may pat my shoulder, and I will see that the tears on his hands chart the end of my time with him.

I continue reupholstering the used chairs to make them look new. It is not easy work, but neither is it particularly difficult. What is wrong with being an architect who ends up re-upholstering used chairs? Nothing whatsoever. What matters is ensuring you have enough to eat the next day and stretching out your hand at month's end for a handful of bills they claim is the reward for your labours. What matters is saving most of your wages and sending them to your family, who will live in comfort on them. They will set some of the money aside to find you a bride suitable for an architect working in an oil state where they extract not just oil but money, pocketing it like rice, as Egyptian President al-Sisi famously said, and as most people believe. Beggars cluster like pigeons around that rice, some of them begging in person and others online, like the sick person seeking money for medical care or the foreigner without enough to eat. The well-to-do ignore these appeals, while the simple people rush to the rice, the flocks of pigeons growing larger by the day. What matters is to fool yourself and mock yourself at the same time, although you can't tell the difference, since they're equally galling.

Though this batch of chairs is practically new, they were sent for reupholstering because the entire house is being renovated and redecorated, perhaps to lift its owners' mood. Maybe their boredom has depressed them. Here I go again, fooling myself and mocking myself at the same time. I have been changing rooms for five years now without gaining any more space. The largest room I have lived in was three metres by four, and I shared that vast expanse with a host of stories. Each man carried his story in his eyes, shutting them on it every night, or perhaps telling it to his companions to ensure they would get a good night's sleep.

Chapter Fifteen

The Furniture Workshop

Dreaming of home

Only after you have faced death do you appreciate the value of life.

Mukhtar

I want to cry, to smash my heart with a rock. Perhaps it will crack, although the death all around has failed to break it. I look at Abdullah, who continues to rave. I can no longer hear him. His lips move soundlessly as he waves his hands, expressions flitting across his face as if he were talking to someone only he can see.

Forgive me, Lord, for being a mere onlooker who lacks the courage to wear a suicide vest and blow himself up along with a thousand traitors, or to split into a thousand men, each wired to kill a thousand more, eclipsing his own death. I raise my arms toward the sky and appeal to God.

"Give me your hand, God, so I can wipe away the tears of women, children, and especially men, for men don't cry from fear, sadness, or weakness, but from oppression, and, my God, how lethal that oppression is!

"Give me your hand, God, so I may offer water to the one lashed all night by fever with no medicine or sip of water to extinguish its burning embers.

"Give me your hand to strangle war before it snatches children from their beds, beads of milk still warm on their cool lips.

"Give me your hand, Lord, to hide the guns and swords, artillery and rocket launchers, and everything else man has devised to inflict death on the streets.

"Give me your hand and take mine, for I am tired of its weakness, brokenness, and helplessness.

"Give me your hand; I am asking you for help, so give me your hand."

Abdullah pats my shoulder. I swear it is him, not me, who needs reassurance. I look at him and see he is smiling.

"It was an exhausting day. We both need some sleep. I have a double shift tomorrow, with double pay." His smile fades before returning: "It's a new lease on life."

I look at him, at the smile playing over his lips as if the world had not taken what it wanted from him and discarded him like a bit of flotsam, stealing his wife, daughter, father, and the son he had never seen. They all died on the night when the stars fell and Yara's hands could not scoop them into the wooden toy box her grandfather had carved from the Christ's-thorn tree behind their house near beautiful Aden.

I learned a great deal from Abdullah: above all, how to make peace with myself, how to show tolerance, and how to cleanse my heart each night to hasten the coming of sleep. It was not easy, but as time passed, I learned. Putting his hand on his heart and closing his eyes, Abdullah would pray again and again:

"Allahumma, give me another heart, so I can keep on living."

He takes my arm, and we go indoors to join the rest of the workers, who are sleeping like the dead. Only Abdullah and I are in the habit of staying up to chat. Before we go to sleep each night, we talk about our pasts that keep us awake. For me, it was long ago, but for him, it is recent. Nonetheless, he smiles more readily than I do and is more reconciled to his situation, to the extent that I have trouble believing he has emerged from the maelstrom of war. He says, smiling ruefully:

"When you witness death, my friend, you realize life's importance. I didn't just see death; it took everyone I loved and spurned me like a mangy cur not worth its while."

One night, he told me about his mother, who people used to say was not in full possession of her faculties.

"She came to our school almost every day. Everyone knew who she was, and they found her intrusion annoying. She would show up at school before the final bell, her arrival signalling the end of her children's labours. It was embarrassing for us, including me; the other pupils would gossip about her mental state and say we still needed a crazy woman to look after us. Like them, we would have thought she was unbalanced if it hadn't been for all the love she showered on us. How can you call a woman crazy when she would eat only after she'd sent food to all her neighbours, in case someone had smelled her cooking? A woman who reminded us over and over that the Prophet told us to be generous to a fault? A woman who wouldn't touch a single date until she had sent some of the harvest to everyone on the street? When we urged her to try just one, she would say: 'How could I enjoy it when the child next door is craving one?' Maybe she acquired her generosity from my father, who was the same, or perhaps he learned it from her.

"People thought she was mentally unbalanced, but we thought she was perfect in love. We never imagined she would suddenly leave us, that the school bell would ring and she wouldn't be waiting by our classroom door. How could she die like that, without even saying goodbye?

"She told me: 'I'll be right back.' Instead, she was hit by a car she hadn't seen, maybe because she was too preoccupied with putting food on the table. My father was travelling and hadn't sent her the usual monthly transfer of funds. She had no way to know if he was all right or if he'd had a mishap, since there were no telephones or ways to communicate apart from the letters that arrived every few months. She died, and we had to make do with hugs from the mourners and neighbours until our father returned. He had brought her a new dress, which he put away for my big sister to wear when she grew up—although when she did, we didn't dare call her Mama."

"'Never mind; the good die young,' I force myself to console him, though I know it won't change how he feels. I believe that mothers were created from the clay of paradise, not from the clay of this earth. I am convinced that mothers somehow emerged from the loins of angels after houris fell pregnant with them. Don't hold it against me, God, that I think mothers should inherit the earth. Their merciful hearts could wipe war off the map, and it is they alone who can transform bombs into flower petals.

In return, I told Abdullah about my father and how he used to let the Eid pass without buying himself any new clothes to celebrate. He celebrated with our laughter that competed for his hug, and with our joyful eyes that brightened his nights when worry darkened them. So my mother told me, after I had grown up, when she also told me about the worst day of my father's life. After losing his wallet with his salary inside it, he returned home very late, looking as if the earth had swallowed half of him and returned only the other half alive. Worried about how his children would eat for the rest of the month and wondering if he could ever forgive himself for losing his wallet, he spent the night praying for God's mercy. Had it not been for his toughness, dignity, and optimism, he would have given way to tears.

The next day, someone handed in my father's wallet. One of his foreign colleagues had found it on the ground, spotted the ID card, and returned it with my father's life and happiness inside. As my mother recalls, the earth returned the half of my father it had swallowed with a jasmine bush growing in it.

Abdullah told me about Safiyah, to whom his father had engaged him while Abdullah was working in a nearby country in pursuit of a better life. Abdullah went home to marry Safiyah, and she turned out to be that better life. She was calm and loving, just as his mother used to be when she would take his hand and lead him home from school after a rough day of lessons, shouting, insults, and blows. Safiyah too led Abdullah by the hand—toward life and love, toward Yara and Bakr—but she suddenly died, taking all of them with her, even his father. Safiyah resembled his mother in her strong presence and sudden death; for that reason, his father seemed to have chosen her, or perhaps his mother had despatched her from paradise.

Though I could not bring myself to tell Abdullah about Houria, I was not surprised when he whispered: "Forgive her, so you can live," before wishing me good night. He rolled onto his right side and went to sleep while I lay awake, wondering how he could have known my thoughts when I had not shared them. Could everyone who saw me read me with such embarrassing ease, or only Abdullah? Had he really looked into the depths of my soul, or had he merely made a lucky guess?

I take out my phone, searching for you among its apps, and find that a message from you has arrived while Abdullah and I were talking. It seems that the night avenges each of us upon the other without our knowing.

Houria

I know you're sleeping now. Perhaps I was there in your dream? Maybe you'll tell me about it tomorrow—or so I always imagine— since you know my heart will soar with joy. But my heart has never told you how its joyful dance stops when it realizes that you woke from your dream without me.

Mukhtar

My heart carries me to you, and I am overwhelmed by a desire to cry. Do I really have to forgive you to live? If only I could be like Abdullah and cleanse my heart each night before I sleep. But I cannot purge myself of you and your love. I need a blank memory, an empty heart, and another life. I need you; I want to start over, to love you afresh, maybe even more than I did before, with a love that does not know anger, hatred, or separation, that brings me back to you each evening before the streetlamps fade and the roads reach their end.

Sometimes I ask myself: When I left in order to forget you, what if life had thrown its doors wide open to me? What if happiness had welcomed me with open arms, and I had found everything I wanted? Suppose you had not besieged me with your messages, so weighed down with love, regret, and remorse? Would I have forgotten you and begun another life, with a new heart that would not let me down, a heart whose love you did not control?

Perhaps I would have asked my mother to choose a suitable girl from the village and send her to me after a proxy wedding, or brought her here after a hasty visit home, with almost no chance to get to know her. I would have seen only her face, heavily made-up in a vain attempt to please me, but which merely aroused my aversion after it was too late to change my mind. All we could have done was move inexorably toward the tragic life that neither of us wanted, as I silently prayed she would be like Abdullah's wife Safiyah and perhaps pass away as quickly.

I smile, scoffing at my impotence: "What miserable dreams are these?"

The vacation would race past, with only a few days to hand over the dowry and hold the wedding, before I headed straight to the airport to continue my life far from you, its serenity undisturbed by a glimpse of you leaning against another man's chest, leading him by the hand toward boundless joy or dancing before him like a butterfly. Could I really have done that, had you not colluded with my heart to redouble my love for you?

"I need to forgive you in order to live. For God's sake, free me from your memory."

I write the words and hit send. Turning off my phone, I cry like a child who has drifted off to his mother's voice and awoken to find her stone-cold. He cries out but she does not answer. He shakes her shoulders but cannot rouse her. Resting his head on her chest, he sobs, but she does not embrace him. It is not some cruel joke, then; like everyone who dies, she is gone for good. He lies on her cold breast one last time, but Abdullah's voice wakes him for prayer. Her coldness has not gone with her to the unknown world beyond, but has transferred itself to him. He curls up in a ball, trembling.

Abdullah places his hand on my forehead and yanks it back.

"You have a fever!"

Fever is like a sad story. It makes us docile; we curl up like nursing infants who ask nothing of life but the breast of a loving mother. But we have grown up, and our mothers are too shy to embrace us when we cannot confide in them. Tears, not words, issue from our throats. I take a feeble breath but am overcome by a fit of coughing until my breath stutters and fades, leaving me half-blind. I am extremely weak, unable to stand, and I want to cry. Neither alive nor at death's door, I have a fever of the soul. I want to break free, to run away from everything—myself, you, our petty concerns and our grand delusions—and don't forgive me for no longer calling them dreams. Maybe I will quit my job and go home, or maybe not. Life without work makes you feel you are wasting your time. If I return, I will still be hostage to your love, and in the end, it will kill me—that is, if I have any breath left. There is no point in staying here. Maybe I will leave. I really need to leave!

The feverish hallucinations keep coming and the cold compresses never leave my brow. Abdullah skipped work today to stay by my side, giving up the double wage he would have earned had it not been for my sudden fever. Whenever I open my eyes, I see him standing nearby, and I ask: "Isn't it morning yet? Go to sleep so you can get up early for work. Don't forget you'll be paid double. Go on; I'm not a child who needs you to put ice packs on my forehead." I close my eyes to his smile and awaken to it. This man who came from the heart of death is tougher and more resilient than I am. He tells me he only knew the value of life after he'd met death face to face. It took everyone he loved but spared him after telling him it would return soon for one of his friends or loved ones, and he would have to accept it without raising his voice or turning his back on life.

After two days of the fever's fiery scourge, I lean on the wall beside my mattress and pick up my phone. Has she sent a message? Did she worry when I didn't open it? I turn on the phone and am surprised to find only one Facebook alert that pops up before I am ready. My heart races. What has she written? Has she decided to release me as I begged her to, or is she still clinging to me like a light at the end of the tunnel? Will she grant me life, or will she hand me over to death?

Houria

All the doors are locked, I know. There's no need for you to say it; I can see it clearly through the glasses I began wearing after you left, perhaps more often than I need to. So go away, far away; don't look back or reach out to gather up the pieces of me. I know I'm the one who lost you and there is no way to forgive. You don't care about all the sacrifices I've made and am still making or about the years I've lost, one after another, though you once feared a day would pass without seeing my face. The tears that press against my eyelids have not satisfied your thirst for revenge.

Go, Mukhtar, just go. I will free you for the sake of your love that I failed to care for, and you need never know it again unless you want to. The choice is yours. I can't stop you, block your way, or imprison you behind walls of unhappiness that will never bring us together. Good Lord, aren't you tired?

Fine, Mukhtar; whether you forgive me or not, now you have what you wanted. But I will continue to be the woman who turns toward your face whenever the sun sets and your eyes rise, the woman who sees you whenever she opens her eyes on life, the woman with whom every man was infatuated, but whose heart was yours alone. You were her every part, her dreams and all the lamps she lit. You know you will never forgive her, but still you love her. When she imagines another woman in her place, she closes her eyes on the sight. When she cries, she comforts her heart like a lover: "He has only you, my heart, only you."

Mukhtar

Disappointed, I gently lower the phone. "What on earth am I doing? It feels as if this life of exile and loneliness will go on for eternity."

"'I love you.' Tell her 'I love you,' nothing else." So Abdullah calmly sums up the matter.

"What if she gives me the same answer as before? How do I know she won't reject me again?"

Heaving a sigh, Abdullah sits down beside me.

"Suppose Safiyah came back to life, bringing Yara and Bakr with her? Do you think I'd stay here? Do you think I'd let another moment of my life pass without feasting my eyes on their every detail? Would I wait for a seat on the plane, or would I pick myself up and get there any way I could—running, walking, or flying—without another moment of this bitter waiting?"

"Your situation is different than mine. Houria rejected me."

"And she regretted it. After all these years, you can be sure she loves you. Nothing is forcing her to wait for you or beg you to return. We don't devote years of our life to something unless it matters more than life itself. If you go back to her, she will never let you go again."

I am amazed that Abdullah knows—or guessed—the details of my life, but he explains with a laugh:

"When you talk to someone about his pain and look at it closely, it's not his pain you're discussing but your own. When we tell others about our suffering, it helps relieve our own. We talk to others about their pain as if we can read their minds, not realizing we are recounting our own lives in all their colourful details. Every word contains a story, and every story reveals our unresolved emotions.

"Speak, my friend, because most of the time, no one cares what you say. Everyone sees himself in the lives of others and reads himself in their eyes, but he will invariably find his personal suffering in their stories." He chuckles: "If you could see your face whenever you get a text, you wouldn't have asked how I knew your story. All I needed was her name, and now you've told me that."

A cockroach pokes its head out from beneath my bed and I leap to my feet. It scurries away but Abdullah goes after it. Cockroaches are the only creatures I don't hesitate to kill. I still remember the cockroach family that inhabited one of the toilets on our first building site and their forlorn look when I sealed up their window on life with cement. Did they already know their fate or did their ignorance spare them any fear? For some reason, I pictured them as frightened children, trembling and climbing over one other as they tried to escape the demon who loomed over them with a fistful of cement, like a machine gun ready to strike them down. No, my dear cockroaches, your killer is not that merciful; your death will be a slow one.

Why does any of this matter? What matters is sparing myself the sight of these filthy creatures. I join Abdullah in chasing the cockroach that has invaded our privacy. As he searches for an escape route, we trap him between us. I raise my foot: "Bismillah, God is great." One blow, two, three; the fourth is fatal. I look for a gap in the rickety wall that might house a happy family expanding so fast it doesn't care if my size-twelve foot tramples one of its members. Or are cockroaches able to count and remember and love even more than we humans do?

My attention returns to Abdullah, whose laughter fills the room.

"You see? One little cockroach can make you forget all your troubles and start chasing it. You suddenly turn from a victim into a killer. Life requires us to keep moving, because it never stops. Only you stop when you stumble; everyone else keeps right on going."

I smile at my pathetic victory, scratching my head and turning away from Abdullah with embarrassment. I feel like Don Quixote, tilting at the windmill of a frightened little cockroach. How shameful! I will never kill a cockroach again. I swallow my disgust. Can I really face down a scuttling cockroach without summoning my full force and the assassin lurking within my scrawny frame? We humans can't seem to repress the desire to kill whenever we confront someone weaker and smaller. We are only weak before those who are strong or whom we think strong, or when we face those armed with weapons we don't have, who view us as cockroaches to be exterminated.

So it can happen—suddenly and without warning—that your supreme worth becomes that of a cockroach that everyone abhors, and which they are all, without exception, trying to eradicate. Feet both great and small take turns crushing you, competing to kill you, while you have only your eyes that dart among them, and your heart, which knows its trembling will soon end.

Each of us claims to be a good person, but when we find ourselves in a position of strength, we rebel against our good nature and reveal our darker side. I can still remember that experiment at Stanford

University, where students assumed the role of prisoners and prison guards. The students playing the prison guards inflicted every manner of psychological torture upon their peers, their only concern how to perform their roles in the way best suited to their mock profession. When the experiment ended, all the students needed formal counselling to return to normal. This demonstrates how we all harbour an evil side, which merely awaits a chance to manifest itself. No one can claim he was born good, for that goodness will not last when life tears it away day by day, piece by piece.

I am pathetic, forever muddling things up or starting something new before I end up somewhere else. The road ahead of me is unpaved—all my roads are winding, tortuous, as if I were lost in a maze. I always need someone to take my hand and rescue me. I am weak: in body, soul, and resolve. I could not pick up my sword and go to war with your decision; I could only do battle with a small, defenceless cockroach and gloat over its death.

Chapter Sixteen

The Furniture Workshop

Five years in Oman

Our laughter melts away like sugar as our salty tears run over our lips.

I peered down at my chest where Shaykh Mansur had fixed his gaze. I was wearing one of his son's shirts with his photo on it, a gift from the boy's younger sister at his most recent birthday party. Shivering slightly, I sprang to my feet without thinking and declared:

"We'll do it, Shaykh Mansur—all the work that's been stopped or suspended, we'll finish it. We won't leave you in the lurch. None of us is a liar like Mujahid."

My companions gulped with relief, as if they'd been waiting for someone bold enough to make a decision for them. With a smile of satisfaction, Shaykh Mansur took a deep breath, as if his lungs had been starved of oxygen. He came over and hugged me, whispering in my ear:

"I knew when God took away my son, he would send you in his place. I didn't give you his clothes because I pitied you or wanted to forget him, but so that I would see him in you. When you grow, he'll grow with you; when you laugh, I'll hear him laugh; when you're sad, I'll relieve your sadness. May God never take you from me!"

A burning tear brushed my cheek before landing in Shaykh Mansour's beard. I could feel its mark on my face whenever my resolve flagged. My workmates and I raced against the clock, overcoming our impatience and exhaustion to complete all the furniture orders. Sometimes we were a week or two late, but the customers were sympathetic because they knew what Mujahid had done.

Shaykh Mansur rewarded us by sharing the profits among us equally and covering the costs of materials himself. He favoured me in a way I could not have dreamt of, putting me in charge of the workshop and giving me a phone to replace the one I had dropped and broken while we were busy completing the contracts that Mujahid had signed and taken payment for on the sly. Such was Shaykh Mansur's goodness that God had sent him someone to rescue and support him in his hour of need. As for Mujahid, no one has heard of him since, and I doubt they ever will.

I wasted no time learning to use my new phone, charging it, then downloading the apps that would reconnect me with you after a gap of nearly a month. Longing surged through my entire body as I searched for any word from you, though I knew the negative impact this virtual meeting would have on my whole life.

Your Facebook message was no less impatient than I was; it popped up on the screen the moment I entered my password. One message, as was your habit when you had been out of touch for a while then returned, reproaching me as if I had disappeared or forced you to, and forgetting—or pretending to—that you were the only decision-maker in our lives.

Houria

This evening understands how I am yearning for you. It's unbearably long; why won't it end? Don't you find this darkness stifling? Why don't you reach out to lighten it a little or wave it away in uncharacteristic irritation? Why don't you blow up in my face like you never used to? Life doesn't go backwards, and the days now departing will not return. Aren't you tired and fed up? Haven't you had enough of all these years that are gone for good?

I want to live—and only with you. Only you can give me a green light to continue living. Nothing should be allowed to spoil the purity of your heart. Forget about my fickleness that you know; come to me with your heart that I know. I always said you were a child of the sky—your heart is as wide, and you are as beautiful. I know I'm in the wrong—I didn't let my heart speak, and, for a long, long time, I insisted on having everything my way. Now here I am, with nothing.

There are no words to express how tired I am. I am worn out by my endless, fruitless efforts to forget you, to abandon your scent on yesterday's balconies and open the windows of my soul to the morrow so a joyful dream can enter. But tomorrow will not come, and yesterday won't leave me in peace. I won't pretend I haven't tried to replace you with someone else, but I couldn't. This heart that you know, or don't—I'm no longer sure, since everything I once believed true is now in doubt—this heart would not side with me against you. It chose you and rejected me.

Some love is born deformed. Whenever I surrendered myself to this love—the offspring of forgetting and delusion—I came back to you with a remorse I swore was sincere. But I always reneged on my vows and ran away, only to come back to you yet again. When will this game end? I don't know, but I promise you I am tired. I know for certain that I want only you, though I was the one who let you go, the one who lost you. But I can no longer bear it. Whenever I think of giving my heart to another, you come running from afar. You don't give me your advice, your voice, or any of the other things I was hoping for, only endless waiting. You stand silently before me, and I dissolve and disappear; I crumble and am lost.

Do you remember my long hair? I cut it—it was too long for a sad woman—and after you left, I buried my smile alive. How can I convince you to return? Will you believe I am no longer beautiful? I have wilted like the jasmine seedling on our balcony. Should I send my hair to plead my case to you? Will it take your hand and bring you back to me, or will you allow it to die alone in exile? Who will scold me for cutting it? You know no one else will notice. Only you cared; only you would ask: "How is your hair? Has it grown since yesterday?"

Now, after this long struggle, I still don't know how to answer my heart when it asks for you, when its beats rebound without your face, when the sun rises and the little one who dozed off in your embrace each night does not return. I still cannot ask my heart to forgive me for conspiring so casually against it. My hand mercilessly tore it away from life. Is it enough now to pat it on the shoulder and smile that wan smile neither of you knew? Or will we endure a lifetime of silence, when I cannot convince my heart that it was not my decision, that I am afraid of myself and all I have lost, afraid a thorn will grow in my bloodstream and block my veins like death, dissolving this bitter patience in my throat? And so I weep.

Yesterday, on the way home from work, I heard footsteps behind me. I wasn't afraid. My heart fluttered inside my ribs like a bird suddenly freed into the sky with no idea what to do. What a disappointment! When my heart turned to look, it found not your footsteps, but only the wind chasing leaves shed by a lone autumn tree. Five years ago, you turned your back and left, five years that continue to scorch me. I remained alone, suffering and pining for you, smiling when the phone rang in case it was you, and leaping out of bed when a letter arrived that might bear your scent. But you never came.

Why is it that after every farewell, a man does not look back, but a woman continues to lick his remains from her body like an injured lioness who knows she is nearing her end? How can the man continue to eat and sleep, meet with friends and strangers, without lowering his resistance and succumbing to fever, shivering whenever the scent of a woman he once called "my love" comes to him on the breeze?

I grow thinner and paler by the day. The dark circles under my eyes betray me. I am sure that everyone can see my disappointment, and how great it is! Here I am, tapping on the door of your phone, carrying love and guilt, longing, roses, and more sadness than I can possibly measure.

Your eyes that once blossomed in mine and flowered in my blood like carpets of violets did not quell my pain this morning. Who can convince the morning you are gone? Who will dare ask the evening to return? It is only I who would do that for you. The garish red lipstick I wore this morning announced my distress, revealing everything I hadn't whispered to you. I could have spoken when you were able to listen, but each of us chose not to give the other what they craved. Instead, we both chose the most difficult position, and we cannot move beyond it. It was an unwise decision, one that should have been buried before it grew up and gave us bleary eyes and red lipstick too garish for the morning.

Mukhtar

I stop reading your message and turn off my phone to escape the smell of your lipstick. You know I don't like that colour; you only wore it to keep annoying me. You know how to spoil my mood by suddenly doing something I wasn't expecting, like not finishing something nice you had started. It's a habit of yours I'll never get used to. After all these years, I still haven't learned that you were made, not from the clay of heaven, but from the clay of my inner hell. You are the only woman I can't put on the shelf and consign to dusty oblivion.

Wherever I go, I carry you with me. Beneath your arm, you tuck my pain, my weakness, and the unspoken conversations that waver on your lips. You know exactly which wounds to probe and when; you always prefer the open wounds, and not one of the injuries you inflicted has healed. I am tired of your texts that don't stop, of my heart that won't stop, of myself as I wait for your irritating messages. I regret that even here, I still line up our words, hunting for a conversation we didn't finish or a word that escaped me, hoping I will suddenly find it and childishly jump for joy. Why do your small deep-brown eyes contain all our stories—everything I failed to say or you failed to hear? The words I have mastered are all trapped in the corner of my mouth, waiting for you to hear them. I have learned to swallow them, lest I drop them and someone else finds them.

I remember how, as a teenager, I used to write your name on the wall before erasing it so no one else could read it. I wrote it a thousand times before erasing it again and again, always returning to ensure no letter still lurked behind the paint. I remain like a child who clings stubbornly to the hem of your heart, or like a refugee who has known no country but exile. When he grows up, no country will claim him; they say he was born a foreigner and must die as one. But we don't always have a choice, and most of the time we are powerless. As the refugee grows up, so does his yearning for his distant country. When blindness strikes him, he can tell no one that the verdant country in his mind's eye has wilted.

The day passes quickly, followed by the night with its odious gifts. It is not the final day, as it seems, nor the final sin. We are still searching for a sin to equal this sadness and something to excuse it. None of us has to share his visions with his brothers, for they don't watch him day and night, and the growing darkness does not disturb them. Some of them may think it is a question of time, others that it is due to love or insomnia. But I continue to believe in a vision that night slips beneath its cloak—this night when songs and groans awake, when we weep without reason or perhaps hide our reasons under our rough pillows, pressing our faces into them, hoping they will enfold us or swallow us along with our unconscious tears. We dream of very little, and much escapes our notice.

"Never mind, don't worry; everything will turn out all right, al-hamdullilah," we say, trying to assuage our fears of an uncertain future without an identity card or even a residence permit for a migrant fearing sudden deportation. Sometimes I wish I were a poet or man of letters, if only so that I could document a small part of our sufferings—we cowards who fear our own shadows. I would write about the women we love who abandoned us or those stolen from us in return for a worthless handful of what is called money. What is the harm in taking another man's beloved, even if you can see her former lover in her eyes as she sleeps in your embrace? Is she truly happy or just pretending, since she found more comfort in his arms than yours? You'll never know unless she mistakenly calls you by his name, and you needn't worry—no woman would be that stupid.

Write about the war that consumes us and that we consume in turn, like food that neither fattens nor relieves our hunger. Write about us as we glamourize that war, so disfigured by the blood of others. Damn us for not dying of shame or dissolving from mortification, for living and dying like cowards. As the sun prepares to rise tomorrow, it will mock even our small dreams when it comes across them dolled up like brides. Although we thought those dreams were modest, the universe was too narrow to contain them. The sun will guffaw at us, its shaking belly echoing its laughter, as we race inexorably toward a road we know is closed. But we carry on, hoping to cross over the corpses of those before us, unaware that those following us plan to march over our own.

Chapter Seventeen

On the Way Home

Preparing to leave

We chew on the past in our stories as if it were a pistachio shell, savouring its salty tang like the tide-marked walls of our old houses.

Mukhtar

"We were not made for death. We will live together, I promise. The sea you once threw me into became your shadow, following my breaths and rescuing me when death was about to claim me. Now it is bringing me back to you so we can finally enjoy love and peace together."

So I reply to you, ending the wandering and indecision that have dogged me for five years. Instead of socializing with my friends, I go to Shaykh Mansur and ask his permission to leave. Like any loving father, he sheds a tear that he doesn't blame on a sudden speck of dust or draught from the air conditioning. I touch his face with my hand and brush the tear away.

"I hope you'll forgive me. I have to go home; I'm getting married," I say with a mixture of affection, confusion, and shyness.

"Get married and bring your wife back with you. I'll be delighted to see you both here, along with your children."

What a lot of promises I'm making today, as if I were swearing, but these oaths are like a window from my heart onto the springtime. I feel coolness slip into my eyes for the first time since that long-ago day, one I will forget from now on. I am as light as a bird, as pure as the sky.

"I have many reasons to stay there. My mother needs me, too; it's time she was able to lean on me. I know you'll miss me. I'll miss you, too. You've treated me like a son, and I'll never forget it. I'll come to visit as often as I can, and when God grants me a son, I'll bring him for your blessing."

I withdrew timidly and left him, spending the rest of the day with my workmates. Though everyone teased me about leaving, they could not conceal their happiness at this long-awaited news. Even I felt an indescribable elation, a lightness, as if I had laid down a great weight of sadness. The hatred you planted in my heart now seems like a lie. I love you as much as I once claimed to hate you, even more. Oh, you majestic warrior! Who but you could have imposed her presence on me? Who but you could have stormed my battlements unopposed, as I surrendered my standard for her to flaunt as she pleased? My child who grows up, but doesn't, who blazes with femininity but beguiles me with her innocence.

I had only recently filed a complaint against Kumar Kapoor for holding onto my passport. One of Shaykh Mansur's acquaintances helped me get back the passport, as well as a residence permit. I hadn't known I would need a passport so quickly. If not for his help, I would have been frantic, with no idea how to get home.

I booked a one-way ticket—all I needed to return to you—and transferred my remaining savings, keeping just enough money for five more days of an exile that was no longer voluntary, and sending a scan of the ticket to reassure you.

"You'll find me at the airport in my wedding dress. I'll invite the registrar so he can marry us there. From now on, there isn't a moment to waste. I'll bring my father and your mother Um Mukhtar; they've been waiting for this moment forever. I'll say goodbye to you now and go tell them the good news. Then Um Mukhtar and I will go to pick out the wedding ring and dress. I don't need all the things other girls run after, like new clothes and jewellery. You are all I need;

once I have you, I will have everything. I promise I will never lose you again."

Your message brings a smile to my lips as your face joins the stars appearing in the night sky. My workmates go out, and I stay with Tawfiq, my new roommate. We have had the room to ourselves since Abdullah went home to make a fresh start, after telling us:

"In spite of the love I've found here, I'm tired of living abroad like a gypsy. I'll build a new house after I've done my part to defend my country and stabilize it. Staying here won't put out this fire in my chest." Abdullah departed, leaving Tawfiq and me in a room the size of every other room I had occupied in this country, as if the dimensions had been spelled out in my original work contract.

Tawfiq had fled his country two years after his wife Mariam disappeared. They searched everywhere but found no trace of her, as if the earth had split open and swallowed her up. His father-in-law took his children for their grandmother to raise in the hope that she could compensate for their mother's inexplicable absence.

When Tawfiq had first arrived in Oman, he was like someone delirious with fever. Before he fell asleep each night, he would hunt in vain for his wife's face. Yet the moment he slept, she would haunt his dreams. It was no simple matter for a woman—a loving wife and mother—to suddenly vanish from her home; her husband would be beset by doubts and suspicions.

"The days after her disappearance were sheer hell, between my worry for her and the bewildered eyes of my children. You can't imagine the first two days, when I had to sit there helplessly while the police searched for her fruitlessly. It was as if she hadn't existed two days earlier, as if her name and photo, her fingerprints, all traces of her had been erased from everywhere but the civil registers. Two days of not knowing if she was all right, whether she would return or tell anyone where she was. Her phone was switched off, and she had gone out in her housedress, not even wearing her abaya. Our youngest child would not stop crying. No bottle of formula could stop his craving for the warm milk she had lavished upon him without fearing it would dry up or her breasts become sore. Our oldest daughter Sara was eleven at the time. She swore she had seen her mother leave the room. When Sara asked where she was going, her mother replied:

"'My dear, you know a diabetic has to use the toilet sometimes. Go to sleep, sweetheart.'

"All these things sent me into a tailspin, with no beginning to help me understand what had happened and no ending to close the door Mariam had opened. Where could she have gone? Was it time to tell the police she was missing? But was she really missing? Had she been kidnapped or had she left the house willingly? She had left on a clear, moonlit night, its sky marred only by a single star which drifted off before dawn, its light waning and falling to earth, which devoured them both before descending into a slumber unbecoming of the bearer of life and mankind.

"After I contacted her family to ask about her, they took over our house, denying they knew anything that might give me hope or calm my shattered nerves. They watched my every move as if trying to read my silence, thinking I might be hiding something from them. How could I convince them I knew even less than they did, less than our children, who woke every morning to her absence? Mahmoud wailed as he searched for her breast, first with his mouth, then his hands and eyes, and finally with his sobs. He woke his siblings but did not rouse his mother from her gloomy absence.

"I don't understand how Mahmoud could have meant so little to her. He used to inhale her scent at dawn and play with her fingers like coloured soap bubbles, though her sparkle was greater. Whenever he wanted her, he would crawl toward her through the sunlight, tugging on her dress until she picked him up, to his delight, or turned her back on his tears until her maternal love forced her to relent.

"But leave aside Mahmoud. What about our first-born, Sara, who was on the brink of womanhood? Mariam had hinted that Sara was maturing early, starting her periods when she was only eleven, as Mariam had. Who but her mother could congratulate her and give her the advice she so badly needed? Whose warm voice and hug will reassure Sara now?

"And me, had she not thought about me? Didn't she ask what would become of the man who worshipped the ground she walked on, as if she were a mythical queen around whom one gathered only to witness her beauty and fill his eyes with her angelic features, like a stray cloud that all can see but none can touch?

"His eyes bulging, my father-in-law raged and stormed. 'Are we just going to stand around while we wait for news of my daughter? It's like she was swallowed up by the earth or kidnapped by a rebel jinn to add to his collection of princesses and houris.' Had he been able to, he would have torn my eyes out before I could tear them from the wall covered with Mariam's pictures.

"We informed the police, but the days continued to taunt us with her absence. As soon as he heard about his daughter's disappearance, my father-in-law took our children, and I couldn't stop him. But who would explain to Sara that her budding femininity had no mother to nurture it? Who would prepare Mahmoud's milk when he woke and his mother wasn't there? After two years, the police closed the case as unsolved, and I came here. Can you believe it? For two years, no one could solve the mystery of her disappearance. The police told me privately that I could obtain a death certificate for her, but I refused."

So Tawfiq finishes telling the story of his family and wife, who may be alive or dead, wandering the earth or resting somewhere deep inside it.

Tawfiq takes my hand, or I take his, and we dash through the market filled with foreigners. Soon I will no longer be one of them. My laughter will echo through our third-floor apartment that faces Hagg Abd al-Halim's grocery. His real name is Abd al-Alim, but people call him Abd al-Halim since he is forever singing along to the songs of Abd al-Halim Hafez as they drift from the old tape player. I will greet the vegetable seller and buy some of his goods for my lunch. I will leave a laugh at the club where I once worked out in a futile attempt to build up my muscles, and deposit another on the ferry carrying Houria and me across the Nile.

I will leave my laughter everywhere, not begrudging it to the vendors of grilled corn who line the Corniche. I will eat Haggah Aliyah's wonderful kushari that famished workers and passersby flock to, tipping her with a laugh as tender as her eyes. I will play a game of cards in Hagg Basyuni's coffeeshop and share my laughter with Ibrahim, the waiter who quit school after just a few years and started working at the coffeeshop to support his sisters and widowed mother. I won't forget to put some money on the table for Ibrahim before I leave. And lastly, I will go by the bookshop to buy some real books, since my eyes hurt from reading online.

The men flogging leather shoes, bony fish, and used clothing—I will pass by them all without buying a thing. They used to look at me askance; I bet they could sense the happiness I was hiding for fear they would steal it.

Tawfiq and I buy some food for our supper and leave. I take the ticket out of my pocket and feel its warmth. I clutch it in my hand, afraid it will drop away like so many memories of the past five years, which passed like my entire lifetime. And, as if the universe were an infinite void, everything vanishes from my field of vision—buildings, streets, cars—leaving only your face and my hand joined with Tawfiq's, our supper in one hand, a ticket to cross over to life in the other.

Nothing disturbs my serenity except the thing heading toward me. I can't describe it—it resembles a mythical bird, like the roc my mother saw in her dream two nights ago, though it has no wings. It is akin to the sun, but it does not recognize time or sunrise or sunset. Whether it is alive, I cannot say, but I am sure it is moving at a speed beyond my grasp. Though people once thought me shrewd, quick-witted, a fast learner, I stand here now like an imbecile, waiting for it to slap me awake.

How on earth do I get it out of my mind? I mean, how do I make it forget me, this thing concerned only with me? If only somebody would answer! I feel the blood rushing to my head to wake it, racing like an unstoppable flood, taking with it all the life, memory, and hopes it meets on its way. Even you, I saw it sweep you away, together with my mother, my father, our neighbourhood that the government has begun to renovate and repossess by convincing the residents it is a historic district, and our history must be preserved. Since when was history more important than people and the present?

The government promised the local people they would get compensation and new homes, and some residents accepted this in the belief that they would receive more modern houses. But they forgot we cannot change our skins, and that, in these new homes, they would not find their laughter, their hopes and joys, or their children's youth. They forgot that the pictures they hung in their new homes would have no warmth, even if the walls were painted in sparkling colours to make people forget their faded old walls, so cold that just touching them made you shiver.

Why do we hang on to the past, extracting from it a life closer to death, even when we are sure it will bring great pain? We chew on the past in our stories as if it were a pistachio shell, savouring its salty tang like the tide-marked walls of our old houses. My God, how beautiful those walls were, so much more beautiful than these so-called new walls, where we can't find the laughter we once forgot on the balcony overlooking that of our neighbour Am Abd al-Razzaq.

Since God had not blessed Am Abd al-Razzaq with children, he adopted us. He treated us like his own flesh and blood, calling each of us "my son", and we competed to help him and his wife Khaleh Karima. He was like a walking sweet shop, his pockets filled with every candy imaginable, their capacity so great that we would dash toward him the moment he beckoned. Though we all knew we would get what we wanted, still we raced each other in the belief that whoever got there first would get the most love and the biggest hug. Khaleh Karima would get upset at the way we crowded around Abdul Razzaq whenever he returned late from work, reproaching us that he needed to rest after a hard day's labour. At the same time, she would slip something into each of our pockets, whispering: "Don't tell your friends; this is just for you." After we left, each of us found the same sum in his pocket, a fortune not to be squandered for any reason.

My mother will no longer send a plateful of our lunch to our neighbour Um Ismail because her son did not like the meat they had prepared for their lunch. My mother used to ask if she could send over some of our food so the boy would not end his day hungry. I would carry it over to their house, making sure to eat some on the way. Before knocking on their door, I would wipe off the plate and my mouth, concealing my theft by rearranging the food to look untouched. Last of all, I would wipe my hand inside my back pocket to hide any trace of my crime. Lest a stray grain of rice betray me, I would keep rubbing my face with my hand until Um Ismail finally closed her door. Once I could no longer hear her calling God's blessings and rewards down on my mother, myself, and all my siblings, I would know she was enjoying our lunch.

Voices collide inside me. Do I know them or are they unfamiliar? What's certain is that most of them are male. Only one female voice—yours—runs toward me, its terror preceding it. I can't hear my mother amidst the racket. She must have delegated her prayers to you; she knows only you can inject life into my veins, so she has sent you while she watches from afar, her prayers still fresh: "I commend you to God, for nothing we commend to Him is ever lost", as she tries to convince the green prayer mat she brought back from the pilgrimage seven years ago that she is calm and confident, not shaking anxiously or hiding her tears with trembling hands.

My little mother, so unlike any other in the universe, was thirteen when she married my father. He used to say: "When we got married, she brought her toys with her." This put him in a quandary: should he treat her as a wife or as a child? He decided she would be his child, and when she reached womanhood, his wife. He used to bring her two gifts: a toy and a short dress. When she showed delight at the toy, he would join in her games. When at last she blushed shyly at the maroon dress, he knew she no longer regarded him as a father, so he embraced her as wife and lover. In spite of their poverty, she remained his pampered child. From him she learned how to nourish us with love when we were hungry and he was away earning a living that sometimes arrived far too late. Though my father's patience might run short, my mother's was always limitless.

My father constantly advised us to be like our mother, an inexhaustible bundle of love, and she in turn urged us to be like him, carrying love wherever we went. I was incapable of being like my mother, and I never resembled my father, who asked with great affection whenever he went out, 'What shall I bring you?' before joyfully returning with what we'd requested. But time and circumstances have not allowed me to be like either of them.

Chapter Eighteen

The Last Crossing

Mukhtar reflects

Like a bubble popped by the breeze, we reach our end.

I close my eyes as I cling to life. Maybe I will wake up to find it is only a bad dream and thank God, calming my thumping heart with my hand and letting my breath come and go as it pleases. Still, I know I am just a number to be deleted, superfluous, like all of us. The universe wants to decrease our numbers to lighten the earth's load and make room for others as innumerable as the nations of Gog and Magog after God released them from behind their wall.

"You are surplus to the universe," a familiar voice inside me whispers. "When you die, it will replace you." Have you ever heard that the world's population was decreasing? Of course not; the number of people is always growing. The sky mourns no one's death, and the earth accepts all corpses without distinction, granting each the same space. It is man who oppresses his fellow man, and there are many oppressors, burying people in mass graves or beneath the ruins of their homes. The dead may find someone who will grieve for them a few days or months before he forgets and carries on with his life—laughing, eating, sleeping, or occasionally crying for reasons that seldom include you. But perhaps—somewhere in a dark room—a heart still lights up at your memory.

The numbness rises to my head unopposed. You arrive, like an unfulfilled wish, an unshed tear, a hand I cannot reach. Terrified, I search for your breast to rest my head. Your legs give way, and I watch you slump to your knees, the ground reverberating beneath you as if it cannot bear your weight. You seem weighed down by me, incapable of repulsing or embracing me.

You collapse.

"It's too soon for you to die. How will the day taste without your voice? How will I eat my breakfast without seeing your face? How will my lips savour 'good morning' if you cannot hear it? How can I bid you farewell and allow your absence to eat away my life? I believed you when you promised to come back, but you never did. I never expected that five years would snatch away our entire lives; five years that were but a gateway to your final departure; five years I thought would end with your return to me."

I watch you fall, and I weep. I am forced to close my eyes. Something grabs my hand and pulls me far away into pitch blackness where I can see everything, every moment of my past. Was the moment they tore me from my mother's womb like now, when I am being wrenched from her spirit? Mother, I cannot imagine the pain you will feel once I am gone, but I urge God to lighten your sorrow, and please ask Him to grant me forgiveness and mercy. I ask Him to fill your heart with my best memories and send me in a thousand kisses that I'll place on your brow each night before you sleep. I ask to visit you in your dreams. When you are missing me, I will come as a child, a flower, or something we both hoped I would become.

May God bring me back as a child who plants flowers on my grave, which naughty children uproot and I replant as a berry bush from which you make your favourite jam, or as a violet to mollify you on Mother's Day when I forget to kiss you. I know you've hated that day ever since my friend Muhsin ran to embrace his mother during the school fete and fell, along with his kiss, never to get up again. If I find him in paradise, I'll give him your greetings and my kisses.

Oh, Mother, if only God would bring me back as an Arab leader who doesn't kill his citizens, attack his neighbours, or take food from the mouths of the poor; a ruler who sees in his people the image of his own small children, finding in their laughter the secret of his happiness, and in their joy, his salvation from hellfire. If only God would bring me back as a bedtime story for children in their graves or as a song to sooth their sad tears, as an angel to guard them while they play, or as pieces of brightly coloured candy that sweeten the tongue. If only He would recreate me as the laughter in their beautiful faces and sunken eyes or as a mother who does not die. It is not beyond His mercy and generous heart to turn me into a bird that lifts those children up to heaven where He can give them new life, or as a heart that becomes an olive tree whenever a child cries, a breast to comfort children when some fool fires a random bullet, or a house to hold the fearful and those fleeing death.

Am I asking for too much? Then I will return as a coat for the girl hunting burnt matchsticks to learn the meaning of fire and warmth or the boy who sleeps on the pavement, waiting for a crust and dreaming of a coat for the long winter.

I reach my hands into the darkness, hoping to touch my mother's shoulder and comfort her or wipe away the tears I cannot prevent. My body is slackening, losing all sensation. The one thing I still have is my return ticket.

Weeping, my late father reaches out his hand to me:

"It's not time yet, Mukhtar; there's no need to hurry, my son. I miss you, but I can wait. Don't rush here to please me. I'm already happy with you; I have been ever since you arrived on this earth. Don't come here—those who come never go back."

Scenes race past as if I am living them; they flash by, except for you. You are falling, and my heart is falling with you. Am I really going to die and leave you with the path, the thorn and the rose, the wishes and the stumbles, the long night, and whatever you want of the dream we finally shared? I can't decide which is more painful— that I am dying or you are staying—but I know we are both leaving this story with nothing, letting it reach a conclusion we neither planned nor expected. We could not have imagined we would both fall, unable to reach out and catch each other, or that my life would finish here, far from everything I love, as alone as the day I was born.

Did you expect our story to end this way? And I? Would I have come here if I had known the ending began here, if I had known I was crossing, not to a new life, but to my death?

Oh, the irony of fate! I want to laugh, no—cry, no—laugh, no— cry. I no longer know how I feel in this moment that won't end, as if I am living a whole second life in the blink of an eye.

I am afraid and resigned, weak and defeated. I have been deceived by everyone: by time, by life, and most of all, by myself. I am deeply confused, unable to absorb this lethargy that is suddenly overtaking my soul. I no longer feel pain. I think of my hand; will I grow a new one? It doesn't matter. I don't need another hand or another heart; I want only the heart you once broke; I want it filled with you as it is now.

It is time for me to go. I can no longer choose my destiny as you once claimed I could. I will die as alone as I was when I first left, surrounded by people in the aeroplane but alone among them. Perhaps now someone else is dying, a star is flickering out, a flower is wilting, but they will not keep me company on my unknown journey. How many birds are choking on their song? How many graves are being dug, how many filled? How many candles are being lit for the departed, how many coffins covered with earth? How many prayers are recited for the dead, and how many mourners march in their funerals?

The worst thing about death is that you can't join your loved ones in crying for yourself or dry their eyes before a fresh bout of weeping overcomes them. You can't watch them collapse or embrace them to soothe the grief that burns their hearts. You die, but you don't take your sadness with you. Instead, you leave it to be parcelled out with the rest of your legacy of love and money—if there is any money, that is. You die knowing that nothing will outlast you for long. Your memory will fade and all your loved ones forget you, though they may mention you in their morning salutations and ask God to grant your soul mercy. Someone may mention you in a text to his loved ones, the message reaching friends across the globe before bouncing back to you, its circle widening before it narrows.

They will gossip about you for a long time, but a day will come— before you're ready—when they drop you from their morning conversations and pour your name away with the dregs of their coffee. Perhaps you travelled to work with someone in the mornings, but you won't return with him in the evening, for the sun is too hot for any memory that doesn't cool and soothe the heart. Nothing lasts for long: so life has taught you, and so your death will teach them.

Mukhtar, my good friend. The voice inside me reappears. My friend whom I thought was me until the moment of the impact. Thirty and more years ago, when you were only a gleam in your mother's eye, did you know you would enter life and leave it on identical days—the sky cloudless, with no sign of rain? That you would be born and die in the evening, as if the daylight wanted to disown you and cast you off in order to continue? You find that strange, you who always kept the lights on because you were afraid to sleep in the dark. You thought darkness brought longing, and nothing is more frightening than a heart consumed by longing. You feared the souls of your loved ones that no longer come to you unbidden; you feared you would die in the dark, unseen. Your prophecy has come true, my only friend—and yet it hasn't. Here you are, dying in plain sight, yet no one reaches out to embrace you. Haven't I told you that nothing in life is perfect? We don't always get the things we run after, and everything we cry over was created only to make us weep.

Don't be sad, my friend. You couldn't have imagined an ending more tragic than this; it's even worse than you expected. The lights have been switched on for you, and maybe you'll be in the newspapers tomorrow. Even if they don't publish your name, they'll be sure to mention the foreigner who dreamt of a return to his homeland and his beloved until Death insisted on snatching him away.

Just like that, in a moment of joy, everything ends, without appointment or prior warning—like a dream that finishes before you wake, a bubble popped by the breeze, a cloud sailing through an empty sky. We die as if our hearts had not been entwined, like moths drawn to a lethal flame. We die as if we had been only a void, leaving no trace of ourselves for those on the same path.

Everything comes to a stop. The lights are no longer running. The pounding of your frightened heart subsides. You will not see your mother pray or hear your Houria weep on your breast as she whispers: "I've missed you so much. When will you return?"

Badriya Al-Badri

Author

Badriya Al-Badri is an acclaimed poet, novelist, children's author and educator whose work has been recognised far beyond her native Oman. In 2021 she was the first woman to win Qatar's prestigious Katara Prize for Poetry, earning the accolade of "The Prophet's Poet". Her 2018 novel *The Shadow of Hermaphroditus* was chosen as Oman's best novel in 2019. In 2022 Saqi Press published her novel *Fombey*, which deals with Belgian colonization and slavery in the Congo.

Al-Badri has authored numerous award-winning collections of poetry and prose for children and young adults. She is active in developing children's literary potential, directing Oman's initiative "I imagine and write" to encourage young writers, and is the former editor of the children's literature column in Murshid magazine. *The Last Crossing* is Al-Badri's second novel.

Katherine Van de Vate

Translator

Katherine Van de Vate translates modern Arabic fiction into English. Before embarking on translation, she served as an American diplomat in the Middle East and as a Near East curator at the British Library. Her translations have been published in Words without Borders, Asymptote, Arablit Quarterly, Y'allah, and elsewhere.